Short, Long, and Longer Short Stories

By

Richard F. Jarmain

authorHOUSE™

1663 LIBERTY DRIVE, SUITE 200
BLOOMINGTON, INDIANA 47403
(800) 839-8640
WWW.AUTHORHOUSE.COM

First published by AuthorHouse 03/19/05

ISBN: 1-4184-0068-8 (e)
ISBN: 1-4184-0069-6 (sc)

Library of Congress Control Number: 2004091632

Printed in the United States of America
Bloomington, Indiana

This book is printed on acid-free paper.

Author's Publications:

Poem Book: *Poet's Modern Poet "Human Exposure"*

Novel: *Saltwater Run: Adventure at Sea*

Anthology: *Short, Long, and Longer Short Stories*

Anthology: *Thirteen Stories*

All books are available from

http://www.authorhouse.com

Call 1-888-280-7715 for direct purchase.

Acknowledgements

Vicki Larke-	Typist
Jean Metzler-	Publications Operator
Robert Jarmain-	Encourager and reader
Nancy Jarmain-	Encourager and reader
Roni Carter-	Reader
Carol Rowe-	Reader
Helene Landsberg-	Reader and encourager
Janet Riger-	Reader
Mary Jean Erario-	Professor, reader
Tom Upshur-	Artist
Rose Closter-	Reader and encourager
Alice Peppler-	Chicago Editor
Robert De Groff-	Account manager AuthorHouse
Fred Seiling-	Arms consultant
William L. Brooks-	Professor, Queens College
Marion Erario Price-	Reader
Harris Kanzer-	Fellow traveler
Jewel Kanzer-	Fellow traveler

The author thanks you for your assistance.

Table of Contents

Introduction

Time retreats from these stories. Read and you're younger when finished.

R.F.J.

Cell Phones: So Close, So Far

She wore a black lace kerchief draped to her shoulder. I had seen such covers at funerals. Red-brown hair shined through the Chantilly design. A purple petunia was pinned to the fabric.

Wisps of wind came up the street and indirect light fell from the clouds. The black asphalt she paced and the five-story office and apartment buildings that confined the narrow street portended a trench for a coffin. April, after rain, hadn't shaken the winter blues.

Her head, downward and tilted, caused me to observe the short black skirt that clasped her middle-aged body, revealing a smooth bulge from omental fat. Compact and lithe, her body had held child. I felt compelled to follow her bizarre meandering in the street.

A purse hung from a strap over her right shoulder as she began to cross to the opposite side below my window. Her head stayed bent down as if she had a toothache in her left jaw. She ignored motorbikes and Smart cars.

In the middle of the street, her mid-heel shoes shifted, and I saw she concentrated on something, as if in pain, and stopped walking. I became concerned.

Traffic, although less and quiet after nine in the morning, had sped with little exhaust noises. Cars stopped to face her, but motorcycles circumvented the blockage by circling around her, sometimes going onto the sidewalk like salmon intent on going upstream to spawn.

Driving and parking in Paris were competitions using bumpers and fenders as weapons.

She rotated in the middle of the street and looked up to my second floor window where curtains swirled her way. I had been found out, but still watched her—irresistably involved.

So, she also had been discovered because her left arm held a cellular phone and she lingered watching me from the middle of the street. I'll never forget her clear round cheeks, brown eyes, lashes, and hair. She admitted she wanted human contact by being there and looking up to me. Was I right?

Her silken walnut hair with a flare of red tint and her stare became a part of me.

Her penetrating gaze floored me. I'll never forget our eye contact. She and I had lingered in a dilated state. I rocked back onto my heels away from the railing. I was smitten with love.

Nothing seemed to bother her until a delayed green sanitation truck gunned exhaust to entice her to turn and pay attention. Once again the cell phone was hidden from me. She adjusted the pocketbook strap and continued crossing to the opposite side of the one-way street.

The noise and emissions increased as the plug of backlogged cars passed, and a morning calm returned.

I studied her pacing the other side of the street. Her straight legs had defined kneecaps. There was no flab. There was a blue ribbon bow on one of her naked ankles. I had to assume shapely thighs and hamstring muscles as her short black skirt clung to her body.

Two women exited a bookstore near her. Their black and brown scarves, slacks, and cigarette smoke invoked a maudlin feeling of the predictable malaise of humanity—the search for an item or another human or a story—an interim diversion from sex.

Yet, as fascinated as I was by the streetwalker, the balance of dry after wet, of silence after noise, of light after darkness, started to favor me. Light descended from above the parapets across the trench to focus upon the walker so she moved from her side into the deeper shadow of my side of the street.

As she passed, left to right, below my French window, she started another conversation on the cell phone. Had she locked herself out of her apartment? Did it exist? How was it furnished? Was it saturated with perfume? How could I meet her?

As I looked down, her broad shoulders made a cross out of her. Her legs were bare skin—all cream. Sinewy ankles and a hand moved out and in from her body during the walk fifty feet up my sidewalk. She turned and looked up to me.

I was embarrassed because I was leaning over the iron railing, and she caught me studying her once again. She stared at me. What should I do? The pangs of sexual attraction clamored inside me.

It was too late to signal her because she entered the middle of the street, ignoring the little Renaults and bikes. Was her phone reception better in the middle of the street? Whom was she calling?

She held her poise again, rotated, and now her face was clear and cherubic, one painted by Gustave Courbet in the nineteenth century. The chrome phone held to her black lace couldn't dispel the image of the reclining nude with opulent black hair emphasizing the natural protection of the conception and birth canal. The nude was exhibited in the Museum d'Orsay.

Was she frustrated, her energy forcing her to roam into the street? She concentrated on her conversation. She spread her legs in dominatrix design. She stared down the street toward the advancing world. I felt she wanted to control the streets of Paris, and sought entry into the lives of people in the apartments and offices resisting her calls.

Thwarted, she was. I believed she walked because no one would receive and talk to her, to start her day in a personal and caring way.

Was her mother ill, and was she telling the doctor off? No, she wouldn't loiter. What could I do?

Before long, she stood directly across the street from my window, only twenty feet below. She was a growing flower from the city grave with brown comet eyebrows, seeking entry into the world of love. As a smiling blossom from concrete, or a rising petal of inquiry, her essence ascended. Who shares feelings through space without talking?

I wished to be Peter Pan, able to fly. I'd gather her up and place her on the double bed behind me. I wanted to allay her fears and tell her she wasn't alone. Would she allow me? Would she shed a tear?

I desired to show love clearly and openly by caresses and kisses on her soft cheeks, by exploring her abdomen and stroking her statuesque legs to share that she was not the only streetwalker, but I also walked, even flew, and had strength, and that together, we would grow important in a morbid city.

Two people, wanting love, together, feel as one. They are stronger with a future. Our search may be over.

She flipped the cover of the cell phone down and held it at arms' length. She walked back again to the middle of the street directly below my window.

Holding up the cellular phone, she pointed at it.

In my white under shorts, I nodded and went to the desk and wrote down my cell-phone number on a piece of paper.

At the railing, the sun covered my naked chest.

I crumpled the paper into a wad and threw it to her. I flipped open my cell phone and waited. □

Slingshot

There is one thought, one rule I've lived by, ever since I was a boy. It is never to harm a living creature—never to strike a blow with the ignorance to hurt. As I got older, there were times—bloody times—when I had to defend myself. Yet I never meant to initiate willful harm to another person.

My family lived at the border where forest meets grass fields in Montauk, Long Island. Our ocean facing stone patio was made from red and blue slates each surrounded by cement. The second floor provided shade and funneled intermittent, cool breezes. My family built this hillside house—slowly over time. I helped. Often my uncle took the train from New York City to assist us. We needed helpful guests. Money was scarce.

One hot July day in 1948, I sat on a three by six inch wood beam that was supported by cement blocks. I sat alone. My friend from Ohio who lived down the hill, had to stay in. My brother was in town shopping with my mother. Today was as important as the commissioning of a steamship would be to its builder. It was the day to try my homemade slingshot!

My friend hid his from his parents. My uncle thought mine was "neat." Here's how I made it.

I had searched in the woods for a bifurcating branch. I grabbed and bent many branches in my small hand to feel it and to make sure the two emanating branches would not flex. Testing took time. A perfect V shape above the handle, that had enough width for a stone in its leather mitt to pass through, was essential. The branch had to be big for my grip because eventually the entire frame would be debarked.

Thin branches were no good. The grip would eventually be flattened where the left thumb pressed against the back, and then nothing would be left. The ends of the forks would have circular bands cut out so the stretched rubber couldn't slip out. I found an oak branch and sawed it off.

I whittled away the bark with a penknife, and then laid the frame in the sun on a flat slate for several days. I put a heavy cement block on and off it, to prevent warp as it dried. The Y-shape changed color from green to yellow and eventually to white. I sanded it with emery cloth. The feel pleased me. The creation of a useful instrument interested me. There weren't any imperfections—in fact at the bifurcation there had grown a strengthening knot—the start of a trifurcation. I knew this made my choice of frame extra strong.

My brother and I had already taken the inner tube of a bike tire, laid it out, and used a roofer's tin snips to cut strips of straight, flat rubber.

To get a pencil outline near the fork tips, I wrapped a black rubber strip around them. Then I pencil-scored a ring, removed the rubber, and carefully whittled out the ledges that the rubber would sit between. They'd prevent the rubber from slipping or moving when I aimed.

Our bare feet were brown, callused, and dirty. Pebbles from the dirt roads rarely hurt.

We searched on tiptoe in a closet for Dad's scruffiest and most worn out shoes. Mother didn't approve that we disrupted the closet and cut out the tongues of Dad's old shoes. We had to repeat this search and mutilation because leather tongues with black grime marks under shoelaces or stiff and improperly shaped ones were unacceptable. Most had to be discarded. After all, how a sling feels and looks is important among boys.

We laid the tongues of leather out on the bench. Brown was prettier than black. We polished them with cordovan shoe polish. The more color in the sling, the more it became a piece of art.

Two perfect slits, equidistant from the edges of a trimmed leather tongue, were made with a Gillette razorblade. I was proud of my slits because the rubber could pass through without any uneven tension. Two of us made the sling because the turned back rubber had to be tied in the stretched position. My brother pulled the passed through black strip in front of me on the bench. I wrapped the bitter and standing parts of the rubber with yellow fishing twine.

The result was black rubber, cordovan leather, and black rubber with yellow whipping as joinery. The sling lay passively on a red slate, like a necklace.

What is the right length of rubber? I had long arms. This gave me an advantage over the neighborhood boys. At maximum extension I could be devastating.

I had only one chance at cutting the length or I would have to start over. I still had to help my brother make his.

So I held the sling to the unvarnished Y frame. I pulled lightly holding the rubber against the wood arms.

Calculating the final cut of rubber is crucial for maximum force, comfort of feel, swiftness of loading, and for projecting the stone. I thought, and I did it. I cut the black strips longer than my normal stretch because I knew I would grow.

While holding the frame and sling, I noticed that white oak and black rubber were incongruous. Black and white are dichotomous.

I searched out a screwdriver, brush, and a can of varnish. After we had worked together on the house, my father said I could use any tool as long as I cleaned it and put it back. I tried to pry open the lid with the screwdriver. It was difficult. I had to lift up the cover from different places around the lip until all at once I could lift the top. I dipped the entire frame into the varnish with pliers and touched up runs with the brush. Then I took a piece of wire and hung the frame up to dry from our rabbit cages.

Varnish takes a long time to dry. I suffered through the wait. But after two days of hanging, the frame was dry. It glowed— in an amber finish. It was beautiful.

My brother had trouble finding a perfect frame. His had a kink but he continued to develop it so we could finish close together.

Yesterday he stretched each of my rubber strips from the arms of the frame while I seized using yellow whipping twine. I tucked the two cord ends under and between the tunnel of twine so no knot could be seen or felt. "Dynamite!" he said. Then I did the same for his.

"Wow!" we said. "Now we're armed." We were seven and eight years old. Mom hit the dinner bell.

Today, I carefully picked stones from our beach collection for ammunition. My brother and Mom were in town, and I got off the beam and moved about the patio.

I picked up a smooth disc that was yellow and white garnet. I pressed it into the leather tongue like a baseball into a mitt. I worked it. I felt the edges of the top and bottom of the stone through the leather. I used my curve-ball grip—second and third fingers on top, thumb on the bottom.

That's when I looked down the flagstone steps to our well. Its submerged pump purred with a distant vibration underground.

To the right of the steps was a stone retaining wall. Above the wall, on the green slope of the hill, I saw a vivid, robin red breast. It had to be young like me. Its varnished, pointed beak faced the distant ocean. It looked innocent—pure.

The bird intensely gazed south against the slight prevailing salt air. Its anticipating face looked smart and happy.

The tongue and stone were one. I pulled back the tongue and black tubing. I stopped. I lowered the slingshot. I raised it back with the brown tongue just below my right eye. I pushed the frame forward, stretching and stretching the rubber once again. The forward-pointing short beak, the intelligent eye, and the red with white breast framed in the V.

Hold no more. I released the leather. The stone, tongue, and rubber collapsed forward. My extended left arm slowly dropped. The flat side of the stone flew slowly in the hot air.

"Thud!" I stared. Three black and red feathers endlessly meandered to the grass. I had hit the folded left wing and chest. The robin still stared south. Shock stopped its heart. It fell on its right side—stiff. Its two tube legs stuck out at me.

My eyes dilated. I approached the hillside. What did I do? What have I done? I swallowed my saliva. Indescribable feelings wormed in my stomach. Thought prevailed. What have I done? I walked closer—tentatively.

The young robin, just as it had fallen over, swiftly reversed the fall. It stood and flew with strong strokes south into the bright, blue sky. It had never looked at me. Neither one of us knew what had happened. Only I knew the flat, smooth stone surface caused the hollow "thud" and saved a life. If the edge of the Frisbee-shaped stone had hit the bird, it could have died. I felt relieved. Harm had been retracted. Death was unintended. Meaning implanted so well, I've never forgotten. □

The Snorer

Five people—my two children, my mother, her lady friend, and I—sought sleep in one motel room. A final review showed my two boys sleeping from opposite ends on a single, rollaway bed. Mom and "Auntie," as we called her friend, were laid out on twin beds like on slabs in a morgue—their bellies bulging. I stood ready to crawl into a blanket on the floor.

Ice cream frappes, loaded with more bananas and cream than anyone should have eaten who sat in a car for eight hours, gave them their somnolent, sugar high. Like drug addicts, they passed out in the motel room.

Auntie and Mom snored in a cacophony of high and low, stuttering sounds. Their raucous rhythms, conjured up a vision of the back of the tongues hitting their pendulous palates—separating and closing as air entered their heaving, fat chests.

Mom had said, "Henry, drive us to Florida," and I had agreed. She had a big, green Fleetwood Cadillac.

My boys came first, and since I was a successful day trader, I closed up my office. Missing a killing on the stock market or a snowstorm in New York City wouldn't bother me.

The women not only loved the children, but Mom's adventuresome ways already forced us to visit several lighthouses and museums along the eastern coast of North Carolina. Eventually we saw an alligator fight in St Augustine, visited Cape Canaveral and the moon landing craft at the Space Museum, and went to Sea World in South Miami, where sharks and dolphins and a white whale amused us.

Rooms were expensive so we all usually slept in one room. Gas and tolls to Florida only cost $83.00—a real bargain for the five of us. I drove with the car in touring mode, which conserved gas. The explorative side trips, the ferry rides, restaurants, visitors' centers kept us busy and tired.

In the motel rooms I was always the last to fall asleep because I had to survive the women's waves of snores. To me this was unique and trying.

Hearing snoring was new to me. People don't know they snore until told. You could put a sound activated tape recorder next to your bed if you wanted to know about yourself.

During the trip I wondered if the cause of snoring was false teeth because Mom and Auntie slept with their denture plates in place. The plates sometimes clacked when they spoke in the car, and I wondered if a plate dropped down to hit the opposing one while the women slept.

Did they snore because they slept on their backs? Their open mouths in a duet showed their pink tongues pressing up and back and their soft palates vibrating up and down, even twisting. The noise vibrated successively or simultaneously—so loud sometimes that I thought the wall light bulbs would break. The pink dentures, palates, pharynxes, and tongues made them look like innocent, fresh babies. Yet, their gross bodies with gray hair could not be forgotten.

One night the boys whispered in the women's ears, "Roll over." My youngsters thought this would stop the rattling. It did. The noisy Zzzz's faded.

On that trip I swathed myself in covers on the floor at the foot of the bed. I was sure I would hear the snoring for a lifetime. I tolerated it, became immune to it, and then never thought of it until now.

♫

My boys had grown and succeeded in their professions.

My wife, who seemed to be content with my sleeping habit, which I will describe, had never complained to me about anything.

Our marriage, ideal until she drove off a cliff after shopping in the South of England, seemed now to be much more important than I had recognized. I had taken her for granted.

Why she died then and there was always a question. Maybe the cause was the traffic patterns in England with all the circles; possibly it was her seating and steering on the right side of the front seat, from what she said was the "wrong side" of the road.

Certainly we knew a Brit by the way he descended a stairway. Most of the time we caused him or her to move over. They knew we were Americans. Could she have been on the improper side of the street?

I do know that it had taken me two years to get her to accelerate to the faster pace of traffic in New York City. She had come from a small midwestern town.

Her accident and the funeral arrangements affected me severely. I became depressed and would not go out. Knowing now what I know about snoring makes me love her more even if it is in thought, post-humorously.

People snore; it happens. Some people don't like snorers if it keeps them awake. If you don't know that you snore, there may be people that don't like you, and you don't know it. Do you think my wife loved me or tolerated me? That is the question I ask myself, knowing what I know now.

Wow! Maybe my wife didn't like me because the revelation is, and I'm in my fifties, that I also am a snorer. This fact has been confirmed. This fate I do not wish on any male. Was my wife happy in our marriage?

♪♫

After I came out of my depression in the United States, I dated, trying to find a compatible companion for my later years.

"Henry," a potential companion said, "you have to do something about your snoring."

She and I were travelers. An athlete who in the past had played on the Romanian World Soccer Team, she also played doubles tennis, a sport that kept me fit. She wanted to experience me in my fitness. I had been naïve and protected from the world by my late wife, who could fight with any storeowner over any injustice as she saw it.

Once in a nightspot, my deceased wife had lit up and yelled at two men who were about to bop me for something. For what? I wouldn't know. Startlingly, the thugs listened to her tell them not to think of doing what they intended. I assumed it would hurt, and didn't know why they would do it. That's how naïve I was.

Now, I learned about the seriousness of snoring.

The Romanian woman lay next to me in a luxurious bed at a seaside resort. I told her, "If I snore as you say I do, turn me over—give me a shove. It worked with my Auntie and Mom. My boys and I could get them to stop."

In the middle of the night, my eyelids opened toward my new friend and I saw a spear in the form of her five fingers thrusting at me in an attempt to turn me over—to stop me from snoring. Something worked because we woke in the same bed in the morning.

This athletic woman always looked fatigued when vacationing with me. Her spark seemed lost, and to explain her dark and vapid appearance, I took into consideration other factors such as sex, but no. She was simply tired from lack of sleep.

That romance didn't last. How much of the break-up could be attributed to my snoring, I don't know. I was very aware, though, of my problem and how it affected a potential lady friend.

Should I have gotten a doctor's advice?

♫

With my next companion, I found myself sleeping on the floor. This was ironically a twist from the days I slept on the floor to avoid the snoring of my Auntie and Mom. Sleeping on the floor was my attempt to mitigate the effect my snoring had on my high-strung lady-friend.

We had a king size bed made by putting two twin beds together at a hotel in Budapest, Hungary. Our room overlooked the Danube River. She said, "Henry, you must have an operation."

"What operation? For what?"

"For your snoring. I can't sleep."

"How's that done?"

"I think the surgeons cut off the back of your palate—probably the part that hangs down."

Oh, no, I thought.

"Every part of me is precious. I don't think so."

"Well, don't just lie there, do something. I can't sleep."

"Any ideas…?"

"Get a dental prosthesis."

That was when I created a hut by pulling the mattress out from over my box spring, draped the spread over and down, and crawled under, onto the rug with a pillow, sheet, and blanket. Once again I was swathed in a blanket on the floor like when with Mom and Auntie, but now my sound waves were the problem.

The sound proof shelter didn't work.

Where do you think that romance went?

I needed a woman like my wife who not only protected me, but also tolerated my snoring.

A lull occurred in my dating.

I thought and thought and developed an inferiority complex. In the peak of life, what woman would warm my bed?

You, the reader, are right, if you've come to a conclusion.

♪

Penny and I chose each other. I thought this romance would work. Our acquaintance was respectful, and she invited me to her friend's gala dinner party.

Before the meal the dining room was as quiet as a desert. After dinner, I saw many arms and fingers and heard intermittent guttural sounds rise above the people. They shouted across the rows of tables … in sign language! They were deaf, hearing impaired, and mute.

Yes, I thought that a woman who couldn't hear my snoring would accept me once a solidly based relationship was established. All I had to do was learn sign language to fit in with her friends. She talked to me sparingly.

Soon after that enjoyable meal I took her on a cruise on the Caribbean Sea in a Tall Ship. Our cabin was made from solid mahogany. The table lights were hand carved out of hardwood and the bulbs gave off a glow.

On the second night at sea, indirect crown lighting uncovered the room in soft light. She lay next to me under a silk sheet. I turned the end table light on to read a novel I had started on land.

"Henry, put the lights out. I can't sleep."

Her talk would startle anyone. It was high-pitched, higher than I ever heard.

"Penny, I only have two pages to read and this chapter will be finished." I signed off. She also read lips.

"No."

"I'll go to sleep in a short while."

"No."

I got out of bed and moved to the sofa, and put that light on before putting the end table light off.

She got up and went into the bathroom. I saw she was piqued.

When she returned, I knew I was in trouble.

In darkness, I went to the bed and tried to comfort her by petting her and saying soothing words, which she didn't hear because her hearing aids were not in place. This worked.

The next night I learned that darkness had to prevail. We made love, but in order to sleep, she had to have complete darkness. Light woke her up like an alarm clock.

"Turn off the bathroom light."

I got up, grabbed my book, and read in the bathroom with the rug blocking the light passing under the door.

Groping for the bed caused some physical disturbance.

Later on she would and did tell me, and that ended our romance.

About women: They are such a part of life and I like to sleep with them, cuddle, and love intensely, but I am forever looking at them sleep. I may always observe them, old and young, and contemplate sleep for them and me, feel at a loss, very mixed up, because ... I make harsh, rough, rattling noises in the night.

□

The Third Night Watch: A Yachting Story

"**Rex,** it's a quarter to three in the morning." Micro whispered and stopped shaking my shoulder through the blue curtain. He waved a flashlight into the bunk so I could get oriented. "I'll wait for you at the top of the stairs."

I turned on the reading light after he closed the curtain. We did not want to disturb anyone, especially Oleon, whose bunk was behind mine. I tiptoed by Oleon to get to the head.

I urinated in my tennis ball container; wet-clothed my face; scrubbed my teeth; closed the door and then my bunk curtain; and went up the stairs to the yacht's deck by the guidance of the "theater-like" step lights. The fog bell that rang for five seconds every minute got louder.

"It's a damp night." Micro spoke as he shined the flashlight ahead into the fog.

We walked astern along the deck walk to the chart cabin. He had my offshore life preserver with strobe light and whistle, and he held it for me to put on. His assistance was the type teachers give at the cloakroom door. He probably had several children at home.

"Let's patrol before I turn in."

I grabbed a yellow poncho with hood.

Along the starboard deck, I looked up at the sails. The anchor light illuminated the schooner's foresail more than the mainsail. The topsail was tied down to the gaff. The inner jib was back-winded. The prow was dark as we walked between the partially lit jib and Dave's below deck entrance. Dave, a tireless deckhand, must be asleep.

The darker view forward allowed me to look northeast. The mild wind had intermittent warm spells, but generally I felt the dampness of the ocean. There were several distant lights on the offshore water. The ocean had succumbed to the presence of men on its roof.

"It has been very quiet until recently," said Micro. "There is a *Sécurité* message on the radio. A channel marker has been moved by the storm and it poses a threat instead of an aid to boats entering the Cape Cod Canal."

"I'll listen. Where are we?"

"We are south of the Boston shipping lanes and north of Cape Cod. Near Stellwagen Shoal. Take the flashlight. I'll go below."

"Good night."

I was alone. We had to have covered fifty nautical miles yesterday. I must have sailed hard. The ringing bell became a part of the night.

Back at the navigation table, I studied the chart in the subdued red light. We were "hove to" ten miles north of Provincetown. Through the glass panels above the wide table I saw that the deck was level or slanted left. The sails changed from wind-taut to slack, but because the wheel was turned and locked to the right, the wind force against the sails and the water force against the rudder canceled out. The rudder turned the bow into the northeast wind, and the backed jib forced the bow away from the wind. In balance we minutely swiveled north, but essentially we were at rest with our sails lit up. At times radiation fog shaded the anchor light, scattering it into the beads of mist.

The noise of the VHF radiotelephone filled the red room. "*Sécurité, Sécurité, Sécurité,*" transmitted as a safety warning from a boater near the displaced buoy. The calling boater used latitude and longitude to mark his position. The Coast Guard came on the air informing boaters of the buoy hazard, and that it had sent a Coast Guard boat to the area. "Shift to Channel 22 Alpha," said the Coast Guard operator. More information was radioed.

I knew the buoy was a very important buoy in Cape Cod Bay—it marked the northern breakwater of the wide canal. The Cape Cod Canal cuts across the Cape to Buzzards Bay, which leads to Rhode Island Sound.

I turned the knob back to Channel 16, which is the distress and calling frequency. I reduced the squelch and listened. There weren't any other emergencies. The chart cabin became quiet again.

I put the yellow poncho on and moved quietly to the stairs. If the radio noise didn't wake captain Red and mate Lori, I wasn't going to wake them. Their cabins were silent.

My eyes took in the fire extinguisher and the Class A EPIRB, which floats free and signals to aircraft and satellites if we've sunk. Behind me on the chart table, the radar was silent.

I said to myself that I'd test the EPIRB within the first five minutes of the next hour. There is a test switch.

Outside in the cockpit, I became a night-watcher. The only colorful sights were the red of the chart cabin and the beige of the side decks and the illuminated parts of the sails. I felt as though the cockpit was a cast-iron tub, and I stood in it. I gently balanced myself in the blackness of the sea. Above me and around the heads of the masts I saw the color gray. The peacefulness of the ocean enters the body, yet the eyes search particularly for lights, their colors and shapes. Ears become antennae to hear below and above the calm of the black morning. With the startling awareness that this concentration brought, I knew the yacht wasn't where or what I had thought.

A ruffle of water slapped against the port side of the hull. That solid tub feeling made me more aware and I became extra alert. The steel hull transmitted messages to my feet. My eyes looked over the rail and the water looked blacker in the indirect mast light. It took on the shape of a black hill.

A humpback whale snuggled along the side of the schooner. It was at least fifty feet long. I could have stepped over the rail, walked across its back, and never touched water. How long it had been snugging up to us, I didn't know.

From the opposite side, I heard a snort, a blow of water, thirty feet out. I crossed from port to starboard side and became aware of a calf between the yacht and its noisy mother, who was out farther. Up away I heard another swirl and ruffle of water and saw three whales. I was able to hear two or three more blowing astern.

The giant black back of the portside whale stayed with me. The yacht was in the middle of a pod. The whales acted like school children in a schoolyard, quietly waiting for instructions. They moved slowly ready to disrupt and disperse if the teacher said it was time to play. Diving was their fun.

The pod moved in synchrony along the sides of the schooner, which imperceptibly advanced, so the yacht felt like an escalator as I walked toward the bow. These whales formed a family that meant no harm. They caused slight ripples of the water as they lingered fifteen minutes as my company.

I felt like a sitting fly in a bowl of plums. I could get up and not disturb the fruit, yet have a good time watching the curved backs so close in the anchor light.

With undulating ripples softly leaning on the silence, they left me. Like the escorting ships in a modern armada, they had surrounded the carrier and kept it safe until duties called them away. There were no depth charges, no sirens, no horns, no engines, only the caressing water and darkness and my empathy for them.

I searched the water. In my imagination I planned contingencies—rather late ones. If that whale had decided to use its tail to ram the boat, to beat and destroy the boat as an Ocra whale kills seals and sea lions, what should I have done? Was I right in assuming they posed no danger?

Subconsciously, sailors know behaviors of animals and don't always act. I didn't see the large triangular fin of a killer whale. These krill-, plankton-, and herring-eating whales open their mouths and like a giant bucket consume two thousand pounds of food a day. They are here to eat and play, fornicate, and talk by sonar.

They are humpback whales whose enemy is high-powered sonar possibly augmented by echoing off canyon walls under water. Submarine and ship emissions can break the blood vessels in their ears and cause them to bleed internally and they wind up dying on beaches.

Their enemy is the radar on ships from Norway and Japan and countries with or without quotas that hunt them out for their oil or blubber or parts to make soap and perfume and candles and pet food.

Their enemies are chemicals like polychlorinated biphenyls, PCBs, which are found in electrical transformer oils and hydraulic fluids now banned; and other chemicals that accumulate in their fatty tissue to weaken their immune system and make them vulnerable to viruses.

I wondered if Red, the captain, had these thoughts as we sailed across the dumpsites yesterday. What chemicals are being released from military dumpsites? Are they merely full of unexploded mines from World War Two?

When I get home I will search the Internet for answers. I'll send inquiries to all.

A night watch allows and stimulates the mind to consider thoughts absolutely antithetical to my classroom ideas, yet they are thoughts very essential to the most complete presentation of textbook material, some of which is incorrect.

If the stars were out during a night watch, I would be searching constellations by sighting off the big and little dipper, or trying to name a star by its relative magnitude.

I saw distant ship lights toward the northeast, which I surmised passed to and from Boston or were lights of boats night fishing or resting as we were. There are times to make assumptions and there are times when they shouldn't be made. Diligence softens the steps to accidents.

I went below, into the soft red of the navigation cabin, and filled in the radio and weather logs. One of the lights on the horizon had struck me as a little brighter than it had been earlier. I had stared at it before coming down the stairs and knew I had to review the horizon. Preventive thoughts such as contacting an approaching vessel by VHF radiotelephone, or sweeping the flashlight across our sails entered my mind. I went up on deck.

That one light among the several stretched along the northeast horizon had gotten brighter and a little larger. It seemed very remote, but had developed a cathedral shape. How far can I see at night? How far must a light project according to the law? The mist had lifted and fallen after the whales disappeared. The lights seemed to be miles away. Was that white light getting brighter and bigger?

I walked toward the bow to check about. The hanging reef lines wiggled like dangling snakes below the batten we had put in the foresail. The strong Samson post was connected to the keel through the forward deck. The winch and capstan stood inshore of the backed jib. There were no lights on the water west of the yacht. I walked back along the port side, amorous with the tranquility, and marveling at my desolate position on the ocean. I looked toward Cape Cod. I saw only blackness. I crossed to the starboard deck by passing between the cockpit and the stairway to the chart cabin.

The increased brightness of that northeast light struck me unexpectedly. The brightness of a Sportsfisherman came at me rapidly. It was a spotlight on a very fast, wave-making bow.

Wake up Red? Move our yacht out of the way? The high-powered fishing boat beat down on us. It was too late to wake up Red. If that speeding cruiser were on automatic pilot and its captain asleep, our "heaving to" would be a final resting place.

At full speed, the black pilot-cabin windshield, a flying bridge above it, and a powerful searchlight in front sped toward the middle of our schooner. I predicted its polyvinyl bow and stainless steel pulpit would crash into our steel hull, and water would pour into our saloon after the Sportsfisherman craft exploded.

Unexpectedly, as the dreadful fate approached destiny, the Sportsfisherman turned uproariously toward our stern showing her bottom like a can-can girl shows her fanny. The close boat reared its starboard chine at me and sent waves into our schooner's side. Both its propellers spun turbulent water our way.

Our anchor light lit up its careening plastic tumblehome and the closed outriggers.

I saw a man frantically handling the steering wheel when I peered through the side windows of his darkened pilothouse. The displays in his console were lighted red. I could have touched his railing. He edged and sped, never throttling back, along our side into the close gray blackness behind our stern.

The monster boatman barely avoided a premature death! He headed to shore with roaring speed, his fighting chairs empty.

I should have trembled. He must have been asleep. Why else at the last second did he turn and rear up? Where was radar alert? Airplanes have alert systems with zones for alarm. Boats need them. He turned to his left sharply; therefore, he had abruptly wakened up. Most seamen turn to starboard. They learn that with a collision eminent, if all steer to starboard, no one will collide. His angle of attack dictated a port turn.

The close gray and distant black ocean calmed. The Sportsfisherman's tumbling, usurping wake disappeared. The waves close to our starboard hull became custard cones—millions of them reaching up, melting away, rising again to tell the coming twilight that they were still here and they wanted to be smoothed by the morning light. They were as upset as I was.

It was near 6 a.m. I had made entry in the log. I tried to remember his registration number. If a night-watcher reads this comment, he will not linger, but move with haste. "Heaving to" takes re-evaluation.

I sat on the top chart room stair where I could see all about. Dave came from the port side and said, "Red wants to know how far we are from the shipping lanes."

I hadn't seen Red. He must have gone to the kitchen from his cabin through the lower engine room while I was topside. I had tested the EPIRB once and taken GPS fixes every hour and recorded them in the log. On the borders of the chart, it was easy to measure the longitude and latitude readings by using a caliper or dividers and to record these locations on the chart. I extended the previous night-watcher's Dead Reckoning course line to my 0400 fix. Then by extending the course line to the 0500 and 0600 fixes, it became obvious we had moved north at a rate of one nautical mile an hour. We had moved three miles closer to lights of ships and danger. I took a caliper and spanned it from the delineated Boston shipping lanes to our six o'clock fix. I heard over the intercom, "Rex, how close are we?"

Red wanted to know. Why was he in the galley so early? How is Cindy, the cook? She could have been in the kitchen, in the space the Sportsfisherman would have exploded.

I ran up the few stairs and out of the chart cabin. The slight role across my upper back from reading at low library tables seemed to have flattened. There was daylight outside. Seeing gray water do a dance instead of peering into unfathomable blackness struck me. Black had become the quiet, subdued gray and beige of morning daylight.

Red cooked breakfast.

"Eight point six nautical miles," I reported.

It was 6:30 a.m. The distance, to him, didn't seem to put us in any danger. □

The Young Writer

On a clear autumn afternoon, I sat on the board seat of our front yard swing. It hung from a thick limb of an old maple. I bent the ropes in and out and twisted close to the ground looking at a water-filled depression of lawn. Clouds brewed in the western sky and I felt another rain front due because I knew twenty minutes later would come another.

My watchful mother let slam the aluminum storm door of our yellow, clapboard house. She walked the gray porch and down the wood stairs. I could hear her question before it was asked. My mother always felt I required more company. Mutually, I knew she needed more friends. It is lonely surrounded by the eerie quietness in an empty farmhouse in upstate New York.

Dad and my teenage sister worked outside on the farm. During daylight I was my mother's company. Mom and I cleaned, shopped, cooked, thought, and reasoned together.

"What you got there, Feather?"

She encouraged me to write, to do jobs, to keep busy, because a strong work ethic—an opposition to idleness—essentially kept her loving my Dad, who had these qualities in abundance. She thought far ahead. Limited she was, but I learned from her that planning and working are essential to success. I handed my notebook on my lap up to her. The kneehole of my blue cotton trousers showed a mud smudge on my skin.

She read aloud from my writing:

> Wood Pewee in a pool
> Beak wet and cool
> Can you perceive?
> Hear the whistle
> Of rustling leaves?
>
> Here comes the ripple.
> Bird down for worms and water,
> Up and flying farther.
> Companion no more.
> How far? How far?

"Feather! Why, it is lovely." She liked to explain and cared. "Birds migrate to Mexico, Central America—the North and South Tropics. As well   people don't deforest or pollute these southern countries will determine the number of birds returning next spring.

"You must be hungry. Daddy and I'll send you to the big city by the ocean. You'll get a proper education and become a famous writer. Will that suit you?"

I didn't answer. We gave each other time. *Where is the Antilles?* I thought.

"*The Greater and The Lesser Antilles sing from songbirds.*" She had educated me.

Mom scuffed my hair.

I smiled.

———————   ———————

After high school and a summer grooming pear and apple orchards, I arrived as a freshman student among skyscrapers and old quadrilateral buildings. Manhattan confined people between an east and a west highway. My only likings were Central Park and the wide Hudson River. I had never seen so many hues of gray, silver, blue, or green water. The river presented a different picture every time I looked. At night I sat by The General Grant National Monument in Manhattan to admire the lights of the New

Jersey side of the river. I wanted to cross and look back at New York City.

My parents, sister, and I had shopped and found me a quiet and very clean room with a semi-bath in a five-room walk-up apartment. A gray-haired Irish lady lived there and maintained it. She had rented a couple of rooms since her husband died. A science student occupied another room. The south windows let breezes swing crocheted curtains over waxed parquet floors. It became my city residence for four years. Eienstat, the other renter, and Mrs. Irish evolved into an extended family.

Columbia University gave me a partial scholarship to study English, especially creative writing. I'd written on pads, loose-leaf paper, napkins, envelopes, back sides of store checks—any surface—with slight regard for its blankness. I stored poems, descriptive paragraphs, and vivid dreams on toilet paper, paper towels—whatever. I became neater on campus and I found myself walking with a notebook that had stories one from each end of the thick spiral-bound and narrow spaced pad. Most times I stuck the notebook behind my belt against my stomach. This freed my hands, but I had had to move my paring knife to the side of my waist.

I thought of leaving the knife in my room, but for so many years on the farm I had used it to peel apples in one continuous coiled ribbon, dice or slice pears, or whittle sticks and pencils, that it was a part of me—like a comb in a back pocket. So I tucked the three-inch blade between my belt and blue jeans.

My classmates were weird. They exhibited high energy levels, emotional outbreaks, tenacity, Jim Carry jerkiness, and actual emotional instability. Insatiability about life aptly described them, and they gave me second thoughts regarding my decision to attend Columbia. They were very negative, always finding fault, and deprecating. Should I have gone to the University of Pennsylvania or elsewhere? Well, it was too late now. I was here attending class.

After a while I saw that the students were serious, hardworking, and I started taking a liking to their plays, poems, and verbalized dreams. I intentionally stayed on the periphery of my classmates, because I liked to dream, to think, and to express myself, not by gossiping, but on paper.

Students, especially a few girls, could suck my core of thought endlessly. They were pests. I preferred being alone. I ate alone. Eienstat liked going to baseball games and nightspots, so I joined him now and then.

One day early November of my first year, I sat eating yogurt at a cafeteria table. The tray with my empty spaghetti plate and milk glass formed a line across my lower ribs. A very pretty girl with long brown hair walked up across from me, looked at me for a few seconds, and sat down ever so lightly, but did not face me.

I became self-conscious and anxious for the first time.

The girl slowly turned as if on a piano stool, and I fell in love. Her profile was engraved and smoothed like on a coin. A touch of rouge, a strike of eyebrow pencil, and fine fingers that put her silk hair over her cuneiform ear, enhanced her princess quality. My fingers and wrist dropped. The empty yogurt container dangled. She had come to me!

Mom and my sister said I was good looking. I didn't know what that meant, or I paid no heed. Maybe I was. People liked me, but a girlfriend? While I dreamed about it, I thought I wasn't in any hurry.

It's true, I got horny, and Eienstat always came up with ideas such as visiting a house, but if I wrote instead, arousal passed.

So I looked at her. I smelled no perfume. She showed delicate features and dress. She was different from Upstate girls who by now would have had me saddling up a horse for a country ride. There was not a rough curve or even an unplaced wisp of hair. I felt like drawing her pointed nose. Should I say something to her? Do I want to get involved? I am here to study. There is a lot to learn. This has to be learned. Is now the time?

Where is she going? The cacophony of striking plates, knives, and forks, glasses, and laughter suppressed my thoughts. Mom said to strike while the iron is hot. My genitals enlarged. You have to do more than stare. She's going. Gone.

I dropped my arms. My elbows came back from the table. My brown eyes followed her long brown hair beyond the lines of students, out the door into the sunshine. I fell in love with her delicate ankles. Her flowery dress followed every movement of her underlying flesh.

If there is any activity that makes a man inhale to see and feel how much space there is between the rim of his pants and his abdomen, it is the action of anticipating a woman. But why I inhaled in class, after the encounter with her, is beyond me. The professor said to realize value. I do. Write about simple things. I do. Become a mirror of life. I am. Greatly describe. I try. Write in a remarkable way. I will. Make your writing a true recital. I promise. Write about what you know … and that is why I sucked in my stomach. There is so much to know.

Eienstat sipped his beer. I had Coke and chips. We talked, but his head always kept appraising every woman in the pub from shoe to head. He reminded me of an Egyptian with a large brow and smooth body. It was midnight.

"Allison, you say? Um. You know Allison and Feather don't go together."

It was the first time I had ever mentioned her name. His idea initiated the feeling that names have coupling predestinations, even personae that may or may not be copasetic.

"Freya and Feather would be better. Vina and Feather sound compatible, but the sound of Allison...."

He was right. Was she categorized fairy tale or fantasy? Scientists handle words, too. Antigen and antibody go together. Precipitate from solution shows separation. This is interesting because although they are in the same beaker or home, they are not together. Is divorce intrinsic merely by the names involved?

"We've been having lunch together."

"You met her in the dining room?"

"Yes. She came up to me, but later, I came up to her."

"Um. Who talked first?"

"I did ... on our second meeting."

"What was that like?" His eyes searched the short, tall, athletic girls all burning energy, doing exposure and existence in a big city. Televisions glared and blared.

"She had just presented herself. Next time I saw her, I didn't hesitate. 'Hello,' I said. She just smiled. I sat. We looked at each other. She was so receptive I just talked. She listened.

"From that afternoon on, we met for lunch at least four times a week. She had such a languid way of crossing her legs, I felt at ease."

"Feminine, good looking, and a listener. Um. What college is she in?"

"None. She paints."

"Money?"

"I don't know."

"Do you buy her lunch?"

"Yes.... Why ask?"

"Friends? Does she have friends?"

"I don't know."

Eienstat seemed bored or else his androgens were working up foam. "You better do some homework, Feather. Look at Holyfield on that TV. Devastating puncher."

"Would you like to meet her?"

"Not really. If you're in love as you look to be, meet her mother. I've learned you can look down life's hall to death that way."

"Let's get back. Mrs. Irish won't sleep until we're in."

"Good luck with Allison," he said, placing a tip on the table.

Yes, I bought her lunch. I had allotted just so much of my summer money for food. Even if my money only lasted until

April, I would borrow and pay it off next summer, but what about next September? That's probably what Eienstat was saying or asking. Who initiates debt? But it wasn't much. She indicated she liked the way I cut up the fruit on a saucer, put yogurt over it, and picked with carved toothpicks. We both pierced the fruit. Her head came up and she looked at me and I melted inside.

She always seemed to read. A book showed the printed page in front or to the side of her, wherever. The wall in the park, the cafeteria table, and a side chair held one of her books sometime or another. When she left, a book was held like a Bible in one of her slender arms.

So she seriously considered literature and art and me. At least that's how I felt. I wanted to uncover the veils of the forest. It was a heavy desire.

One afternoon of the week before Thanksgiving, I started reading the science fiction piece aloud from the middle of my notebook. She was attentive. My mother used to listen her way. Writers need readers, and before this, they need listeners because writers have to read aloud to catch the harsh, or arrhythmic, hallow-nosed phrases and words that gnaw at the esthetics of literature. And she did this. She listened to an extent beyond I would. Mom had said I was very patient. My sister kissed me because I helped her at length. One observation, Allison attentively applied herself to whatever went on in her head.

At Thursday lunch, Allison talked about her mother. She said her mother liked Aliens, Androids, and Acmonds. This was peculiar, because up to now, I was the only person to write about Acmonds. I did want to meet her mother, so I said yes; I would come over Saturday afternoon and read to her mother and her. She said to come up Riverside Drive and turn into Washington Arms. I couldn't miss it. We kissed. It was a reserved kiss, more of anticipation than of passion, because the mind reserves consideration of intuition. But the kiss, moist and sensual, lingered in my thoughts.

———————   ———————

I think I drove the red Chevy down the hill into a multi-apartment complex, which surprisingly had lawns and open spaces, like a rural campus. Eienstat says to this day that I didn't drive a car. I still get headaches and my head hurts if I explain, but I'll try.

Her apartment entrance was on the first floor on the right at the bottom of the road. She had said to park on the left of the road at the bottom in any space among the defoliated trees and brown and green lawn. I did. On the other side of the parking spots, the road looped and ascended to another building complex up the hill. Across from the parking spaces and the ascending road were a few park benches, a water fountain, and a cyclone fence, which walied off a shuffleboard area. It was a quiet afternoon.

I struck the hard knocker against the brass plate, and the maple door vibrated. I envisioned two bouffant Victorian women with thin waists and hooped hips, heavily clothed and jeweled, properly serving tea and listening to my every word. Wistfully, Allison let me in and I sat in an early twentieth century parlor. Mirrors and tall ornamented clocks on varnished paneled wood detailed the room. She expressed an all encompassing, all inviting, all seductive smile. I had never seen that smile, but I did expect it of her. I dreamed about the forest.

The parlor centered a plush, although stiff, seating area. To the right a heavy stairway covered in a trail rug, rose to the upper bedrooms.

"My mother has to be out today."

"I'm sorry, for I wanted to meet her—to explain my stories, especially the new Science Fiction."

Maybe I was too self-centered.

"I've told her all about you. Another time. I like when we have the house to ourselves."

But I had never been here.

"Let me hang your jacket up, Feather."

The apartment emitted warmth from the cast iron baseboards. They warmed the thick carpet, which warmed the wood panels, which in turn warmed the upholstery. Eventually a little water released around my neck.

"You are thirsty. I'll make tea."

I thought so. Some predictions come true. At home she took on a more mature, more profound existence. She liked doing—action. That's why she was so supple, malleable, and caressable. She was ornately overdressed. "I'll read," I said.

"The Acmonds landed on the ocean. A hydropomorphic chemical reaction turned the water surface into a plasmid upon which they walked, gathering their condensing weapons from the ancillary vehicles."

"Biscuit with the tea?"

"Thanks. Someone is at the door," I said unnecessarily, because she had taken upon herself a knowing hesitation that implied conflict. I made story corrections as she dutifully answered the door.

A flying Hydroskimmer is a less general concept than a vehicle. "Be more concrete," a lecturer had said.

I felt a draft against my right arm. Two boys my age ran up the stairs. They moved so fast I only saw one set of powerful thighs in jeans. Both wore heavy black jackets. The rear guy had a silver earring in his left ear. Fan haircuts on baby faces moved constantly. They entered an oak door to an upstairs bedroom. I saw the drape of a Victorian bed from below. A disproportionate clamor lingered their intrusion.

Allison stood at the bottom of the banister. She looked pensively at me in the salon and then mentally disassociated herself from me. She rejected me. I lost her. Her thoughts were a stop and go that I had only seen when car engines tried to combust gas with condensed moisture in the tank. Puffs of white smoke come out the exhaust, and the car jerks, even stalls.

She took her leather shoes off and pulled up her dress. Her smooth knees like piston levers rapidly carried her up the stairs into the bedroom.

Screams and cries and laughter filled the anteroom at the top of the stairs. Wrestling occurred in the bedroom after which drawers opened and closed. Mattresses and springs bounced. Giggles and fast-talk resonated. A momentary silence occurred, and then sounds of donkeys and mules and shrill cries reverberated. I thought of our hometown veterinarian and a breech birth. I didn't belong here. Forlornness followed my feelings.

I put the bottom half of my notebook away, picked my jacket, and slowly opened and closed the heavy maple door. I very pensively, sorrowfully walked down the concrete steps, and crossed toward the peninsula parking area looking for my car. I felt devastated.

There, by the cars, stood a thin guy. If this were a bank robbery, he was the driver or the holder of the horses. He too had a black leather jacket and a fan haircut, but he was a lookout or just a patient guy waiting for his friends. Evening was closing down.

Out of Allison's apartment burst the two guys. They left the front door open while yelling to the thin fellow not to let me get away. I could not see Allison. I wished life could be less violent as in that bedroom and more loving like at home. Or was I naive and overly imaginative?

I wanted to avoid the parking area, yet I headed there. I thought I was in for trouble, which I wasn't prepared for. Upstate, I had been first in long distance swimming. I was well proportioned and strong, but not trained to fight anything but a cow, which only takes a couple of whacks and a shove.

The thin guy said to stay here close to him and the cars. Since I had no other place to go but my red car, I stood near him. He followed orders. I wasn't staying.

I tried to get into my car, but was knocked over by a football block from the fellow with the powerful thighs. He was a bull; his face was red from what he had just done to Allison.

I got up.

"You don't belong here." He kicked at me, but I avoided the shoe by fast footwork. His cohorts surrounded me like a wolf pack. Think of some dialogue, Feather. Get out of this.

The ludicrous person with the earring stepped up, and clocked me with a fist right above my eye. The thin guy cut me off.

The Bull got chain from the floor of a hot rod. I kept my arms up to defend myself. The sun disappeared and street lamps became the only light. Allison, where are you? Isn't anyone walking outside?

"Let's see how you write with broken fingers."

The new, galvanized chain wrapped around the Bull's hand. The two partners stepped aside to give him winding space. Crash! I took the blow on my left shoulder. Strong and covered by my jacket, my upper torso still wouldn't last.

Before he gathered the chain to strike me again, I stepped into him and grabbed the chain in my left hand. I knew this was wrong, because now I was locked in, but it wasn't in my nature to run.

I was right. No matter how I pulled or pushed the Bull, his partners punched and kicked my kidneys and ribs until I pulled my paring knife from my belt.

That's when the thin guy did the same. He seemed more safety-oriented than the other two, and he was smart enough to know not to let my adverse behavior escalate.

I felt his knife. The thrusts were meant to kill. He stabbed me in the front—the solar plexus.

I turned and pulled like around a maypole with one hand slashing out, the other swinging the chain and stifling the Bull. Doesn't anyone come out around here?

Suddenly two of my attackers looked up the road on the other side of the peninsula along the cyclone fence. From that complex and down that road ran a tall gangling youth who looked like a lacrosse player. He did have a hockey stick, and he along with two members of his gang started a fight with the guys who tried to kill me. Sticks and knives cut the night.

I had never seen such an attack. I felt the Bull knew he had to do me in fast to help his partners. He pummeled my head until blood filled my eyes. I stabbed him, and again I punctured him. It didn't affect him. His jacket, clothes, and fat kept my knife thrusts superficial. He kicked while keeping away from my right hand. We both would not let go of the chain. That's when his shoe to my testicles eliminated every last drop of my strength. My legs buckled, an autonomic reaction fogged my brain, and I was useless. The chain struck my head a couple of times as I knelt helplessly. The Bull kicked me over as if I were a log, and ran into the battle by the water fountain and cyclone fence.

I staggered up bowlegged. My gonads hadn't descended completely. The tall lacrosse leader pulled the earring of Bull's partner. Bull stumbled and was hit with a lacrosse stick. He had come too late. The earring with ear attached glittered held high in the lamplight. The thin guy lay in a pool of shining blood. I shuffled to the unlocked door of the car.

I backed up and turned the driving wheel with all the energy I could muster. I passed Allison's door light. What a waste! Half way up the macadam road, a clean-cut black man in a white car with a red strobe light cut me off and pointed to a dumpster. I steered exhaustively into a driveway.

"Where do you think you're going?"

"Home. To the farm."

"Out. Put your hands on the car."

My right hand had been dipped in red blood where my defensive thrusts squirted serum and hemoglobin beyond the three-inch blade. Where was the knife? Better lost under these conditions, I thought. The officer didn't see the red pool on the trunk as I leaned on the car.

He searched the car. He searched the ripped pockets of my jacket. "Driver's license?"

"In my car," I answered.

He stepped back because I naturally went to the front seat to get it. Then it occurred to me that this wasn't my car. The plastic console and molding were higher, more modern, surrounding the bucket seats. I looked at the officer as if I were lost. He saw me stagger and sit half in and half out the driver's seat. He was so clear, neat, clean-shaven, and motionlessly alert. We looked at each other. My ribs hurt; my breathing labored. One eye was covered by blood. He had pity.

53

"What are you doing here?"

Yes, if I explained and fast, I could leave.

"I came to read my short stories to Miss Allison and her mother—right down the hill."

He didn't want to listen. He left me. I thought I had better prove why I was here. I got up and stumbled. If I get to my car, I can get my wallet with my college identification, and I'll show him my stories.

He was talking to another black officer in a brown shirt, only the shirt stuck out at the chest.

"Charlotte, we have a *young writer* here. Sort it out. I'm going down to help Pete and Willie. He backed his white car down to the curve around the parking peninsula. I saw other strobe lights and more people than ever before.

"Hold on, young sir. You're in no condition to go anywhere. Sit here on the curb."

She slowly checked the car. Locked it up as if she knew it wasn't mine. I've got to get to my car to show them I wasn't here to make trouble. My short stories would be on the front seat.

"My car's red." I got up with effort, bent over to breathe better.

"Hold it, young sir. You are not going anyplace without me."

I felt a communication that said I was no longer alone. I shuddered from relief.

"Here, let me help you."

She put her arm around my waist and held me tightly against her right hip. She had to have lost consideration of her spotless uniform. Her face was Southern concern—full cheeks that never needed Clearasil, deep warm eyes, thin eyebrows, and penetrating concentration. Her black hair was plated with the two braids of Pocahontas. I felt better.

I thought we were walking to my car to get proof. No. She directed me through a short path among trees and across lawn. We slowly ascended the road to the other complex of apartments.

"There's a first aid station. I'll get a nurse."

The road was black by our feet. Upper street lamps illuminated her stoic face. The pain in my balls disappeared. Against my side, I felt her handcuffs and pepper spray, radio, and right full breast. Her softness comforted me. I didn't want Mom to know about my condition.

I repeated my story. The officer was thinking. She partially carried me. She seemed to know, as if these fights occurred more frequently than I could conjure. She was never aghast. Actions have results. If this happens and that happens, out comes a result like from a computer. She was expressionless.

"You're a lithe young man. After we have taken a good look at you, you must tell me about your stories."

"Certainly." I dropped down to the asphalt. Weakness momentarily overcame me. Almost to the first aid station, she got a strong tenant who eventually helped her lay me on the nurse's table. White paper crumbled under my back. Phenolics aromatized the disinfected room. Why I wasn't in an ambulance like the six nexus fighters, I didn't know. People knew so much more than I did.

The nurse turned me over recording every cut, bruise, and petechiae. She said she was looking for small arms bullet holes. She shook her white-capped hair in wonderment. The officer and she stared deeply into my brown eyes. Lights out of dark background must have reflected from my bathing tears.

"You are lucky. Very lucky, young sir."

The nurse held my notebook up above my reclining head. It had been at my waist under my shirt all this time. The officer pointed to the gashed and indented punctures deep into the notebook. The stories had absorbed the deadly knife thrusts from the thin guy. My father would be hopping mad. At least I hadn't lost my book. I was exhausted. I closed my eyes and slept several hours after bed-railings surrounded me. It became midnight.

"Sixty stitches. We have two excellent nurses at Washington Arms. A doctor just took a look. Sleep more."

My scalp was shaved in an area where a bleeder had to be sutured. I felt sewed up like a lassoed calf. I had to drive to the apartment. Mrs. Irish would be waiting.

"I don't want to sleep."

"All right. I'll stay and talk with you." A more wholesome black officer I couldn't imagine. "I have your wallet. Another officer brought it up. We are all sorry this happened to you. There is no red car. With time you'll see."

Eienstat still says the same thing. All I see is polyurethane fire-chief red and branches and leaves whipping me before I plunge into the cold waters of a Norwegian fjord. Setting suns and submarines and nude women half whale, half human, flow into my notebook like the ultimate educational experience.

"Security suspected your story from the beginning," she said. "You must not be aware that Allison's mother has been institutionalized for several months. Reports show the quietest time here is afternoon. We associate peace with Allison's absence. We are having detectives do an investigation. We thought we knew what goes on behind Allison's locked doors."

"I don't really understand. All I know, they wanted to kill me."

"We checked. You're at the university. We have your address."

"Yes. English major."

57

"We'll not detain you. Wherever this goes, you'll be needed for a deposition. Seek legal advice."

She treated me well. Possibly the university is more powerful than I know. I mean word could be handed down to police to leave students alone. Chasing paper and books all night may be stressful. Students, like construction workers, have to release steam. They must continue. They have powerful parents too—alumni.

The decision to inflict pain and suffering upon someone, even in self-defense, was awesome—hurtful more to me than even the Bull. "How is he?"

"He's in the hospital. This is yours. We don't go around with that here. I would do something with it."

I knew what she meant. I read the entire legal thriller genre. She wrapped the knife in a napkin and handed it to me. I'll throw it in the Hudson River.

"Here. Put this over your shoulder. Your dislocated left arm needs a sling. Aspirin? Ah! Now, I want to talk to you about your science fiction, *Burglars From Outer Space*."

She sat near my cot. Her focus was complete. She attentively considered me. Allison and I started that way, but here I had a substantial person—a black person with properness, clarity, and precision.

"While you slept, I took the liberty of reading the evidence."

"Um." I closed my eyes momentarily.

"I also write," she said. My eyes opened. "I go part time to community college."

"Um. That's great." I tried to be encouraging. It was unnecessary. Her uniformed presence exactly showed her strength. She was going to tell me something.

"The story presents a problem at the end. Apparently the earth student doesn't want the Acmond to confess that he had an accomplice who is a young writer." She spoke as if she took diction lessons.

"Near the story's end the Acmond is stuck in the conduit pipe in the ceiling of the toy store. His already large fluid head ballooned because of earth's gravity as the student lowered him head first by a harness. The Acmond wedged. He yelled up to the student on the roof that he will not snitch. Siren sounds worried the student.

"The young writer can't have a bad report on his college record. He saw himself as a *New York Times* feature writer some day. The student wanted assurance. The longer he tried to help release the Acmond, the more likely he would be arrested for breaking and entering."

She moved slowly to the edge of her chair and said, "Now, we … would have the student cut the Acmond's glycerin head with a sheet-metal screw. The only place he could pour his guts out would be in the showroom of the toy store below. Your student's worries are over."

She was serious. We … meant police. Was this Manhattan wisdom? Was she a policewoman? What's Charlotte's persona? Do Charlotte and Feather go together?

I started feeling more uncomfortable. I wanted the safety of my red car.

Mom and Dad and Sis, I am coming home. □

Out Of Bounds

"**See**, there he is," said the counterman.

I turned around from the snack bar and looked up to the contour of a trash mountain. The garbage had been covered with dirt and grass seed many years ago. I saw a man-size black fly worming, bobbing against the clear, blue sky.

"See, those are oxygen tanks on his back—not wings. The morning golfers say this one's a flame-thrower. They should know from the Pacific Islands in World War II. I say no. I worked for the New York City Fire Department."

"You mean that someone lives in all that garbage?"

"Yep." His big eyes looked at me sideways, to goad me to think.

61

He gave me a hot dog with nothing. I opened a tough packet of mustard, but declined to take exposed relish under a loose flap of cellophane.

"That's amazing. It's unhealthy to even live near a dump."

"Yep, but only a few guys know.

"Another amazing thing is the change in nationalities. Asians, Japs, Indians, a group of hard-nosed Russians—all playing golf. The Russians don't fit in. They're like professional football players fooling around at tennis. And everything is 'Do sveedanya.'"

"What do you mean?"

"Things aren't the same. Change. Do you know this cute nine-hole golf course is going to go up and over that mountain of solid waste? It will go right over to the wetlands on the other side."

"You mean expanded to an eighteen hole course?"

"Yep." He took the three dollars.

"That's at least ninety feet high!"

"Look, look. See that little garbage slide?"

The big man ably bent over the counter. He pointed with a pancake flipper to the north bluff of Mount Solid.

"Watch."

The human fly came out the side of the packed trash.

"He'll reinforce the opening with a used window frame. See?"

"Wow!"

"Look along the cliff."

"My God! There are white windows ... along the bluff. Soil and grass have been washed away under the windows."

"That's just pushed out junk. I complain but ... and that's another reason we don't get many good golfers. The county politicos don't come here; we should be drawing players from the industrial zones, but we're not. Business is lousy."

My shoe spikes scrapped the stone and cement in front of the counter. A loud speaker squealed, "Number thirty-two to the first tee."

Most heads of the afternoon golfers lifted up from the practice putting green and the waiting area near the starter's booth. Some heads went down again like feeding geese. Warming up is important. Fixing your bag, getting balls, pencils, scorecards, tees, gloves, and ball markers are essential. The starting players clanked and shuffled like covered wagons going west toward the elevated tee box. Two big white balls marked the ends of the imaginary starting line for most men.

"I'm up next." I told the retired fireman.

"Something to drink?"

"Na. I noticed a fountain near the pump house on seven."

"Be careful. There's white foam in the water in the afternoon."

"I noticed—like a milk cream. It doesn't taste like chlorine."

"Right. That's why I say, be careful."

"See you in a few days. I have the Interhospital Golf Tournament in a couple of weeks and I'm practicing with these new graphite shafts. The ball goes thirty more yards, but I'm having trouble with control."

"They're great. There's an old man. Plays in the morning dew. Never completely turns on his swing, but his friends are always buying him brunch. His flexible shaft goes up under his armpit."

"Course layouts will have to change for this universal ball flight. I've got to keep the ball in the fairway."

"That's basic to get on the green in regulation."

"Surely. Bye."

I picked up my carry bag onto my shoulder and across my back, taking on the slight stoop of a golfer. Not leaving a tip bothers me. Interns only make forty thousand dollars a year. I didn't know whether to be sorry for the retired counterman or not. You don't know who owns what any more.

"Nice drive," I said. I tried an introduction. "My family calls me Doc."

We were a twosome. The starter had not wasted time waiting for the late players of a foursome. I tried to be friendly. The tall player had teed up, hit well, and we walked off the green tee box onto the long, first fairway. We went west toward an entrance road.

"Ken," he responded. Abruptly he walked faster than I, snapping out his long legs.

He also out drove me. His impatience to hit his second shot was noticeable. He circled with his carry bag in my blind area behind me. He dilly-dallied. I hit a long iron. After a beautiful plateau and lifting flight, the ball rolled to the fringe of the green.

Ken's mid iron, second shot landed two club lengths from the flag. He putted out for a birdie three. He was very good.

I chipped to the hole and putt out for a par four.

Ken was an impatient two handicapper, which was better than I for the moment. He had not held the flag for my putt. He had gone on, discourteously.

That is how the practice nine went. I caught up to him at the next tee and hit as he finished hitting and on and on. Crack. Crack and we fast walked the fifth hole—a par three. I played to par. Expert or scratch player people say. The pace had made me somewhat nervous. I do not miss such a short putt, but I bumped the green and the ball went short—or—I also would have birdied as Ken did.

"What do you do?" I asked during the sixth hole.

"I sell medical equipment. You need an X-ray unit, I get it. Need a C.A.T. scanner, I get it. What do you care what it costs! A doctor shouldn't care. He either wants a used unit or he doesn't."

He talked on, staccato like, just as he played. "What's a hundred thousand dollars to a doctor?" He then told me a story that didn't make sense. Logomachy, I call it. It was on my mind as I cracked my seventh tee drive to the right. It rose high, up and over the outline of the landfill. Does the equipment or the man cause such a bad shot? For sure, it was *Out of Bounds.*

That is how Ken and I parted. Of course, he did not help find my ball. He continued walking on the plush fairway parallel to the landfill. I used my spikes to ascend Mount Solid. Ken will never know what he missed.

———————

As I climbed, I thought about the golf ball dimples and altering the dimples to affect the flight of a ball. My ball had my name inscribed across the dimples. Dr. Jeffrey Taylor, M.D. It was written in red and there was a red dot. Red meant ninety-percent compression.

I edged the side of the mountain with the sides of my golf shoes just as I had learned in skiing. I felt the height. It was cooler, breezier. Space below as well as blue infinity above, gave the landfill a surreal quality. I gasped.

My clubs, especially the extra long graphite-boron shafts, stuck up behind my neat hair cut, like a quiver full of arrows. My appearing abruptly above the cliff, if anyone were there, would certainly have scared him. But what I saw was unbelievable. Only a few seagulls in the distance were witnesses.

I lowered myself down—fast—out of respect for privacy. I lowered my head modestly. Yet, curiosity caused me to look over the green lip once again. Besides, I was here for a purpose—to find my golf ball.

Wow! Weird, I thought. Nothing moved for a quarter of a mile beyond. Metal vents spiked upward. It was not the green, wild-flower lawn that held my attention. A low concave area, where garbage had collapsed long ago, attracted my eyes. The nude woman with her arms in backstroke position, her large breasts lifted to receive the warm sun, transfixed me.

Her eyes were closed. She could not see me, so I looked and absorbed what I saw as though looking at a magazine. I enjoyed a hormonal rise. Too much input flushed me. She was about twenty years of age. Her long brown hair spread out from a midline part onto a brown rug on a four-foot by eight-foot panel of elm. Her nose was broad. I could look up under her chin into her nostrils. I sighted along her long rolled in thighs and through her

67

breasts. She was a landing field, day marked by her large healthy feet and slender legs.

That is when I heard the "zap" of the two hundred thousand volt stun gun. I read about these while researching defibrillators. It worked. My gawking time was up. Go. Get off this landfill!

The small man holding the stun gun had a portable respirator with a tank on his back. He wore black-rimmed goggle glasses and a black fire-resistant vest. He stood between the girl and me. His facial mask was flipped open to the side. I could see that he was Vietnamese—a small Chinaman.

I put up my hand to say Stop. I was scared. I told him I was a doctor.

No use. I hopped to the side of the solid waste mountain. The last I remember, she had blue eyes and a dark tan. She looked at me from behind the Vietnam man in a vapid, helpless look. She seemed severely depressed. I was frightened. I felt the heaviness of the moment—a person was in need of help.

I slipped twice while descending. If it were not for my leather golf glove, I would have cut my hand on the edges of opened cans and broken glass uncovered by rainstorms. I became very thirsty and out of breath.

I drank volumes of water at the seventh-tee fountain. The pump house motor whined. The water did not have a white effervescence. Where did the water come from? What had I gotten myself into?

———————   ———————

Three days later I said, "It's true. There is a man up there."

I faced the back of the New York City Fire Fighter's jacket. His round head faced the back grill. Sweat made his bald spot shine.

"I've known for four or five years. I've told the police. All they do is look. The night patrol doesn't even get out of the police car. They told me though; they have a 'thermal imager' at the precinct. Some night they will survey the course. Sure…. They just want free coffee and sandwiches. They are excellent placaters."

"They probably have more important functions."

"Sure. What's more important?"

"Well, maybe they think someone is walking up there. I climbed up there three days ago. We are free to walk where we want." I did not tell him what I had seen. My heart pounded. What was my tee-off time today?

The counterman turned and faced outward to a fence. "See that fellow over there—the military-looking one with the crew cut? He's been up there for the last two days. He is very dejected. Moribund, they say in the firehouse. All he eats is potato chips. He walks across the fairways to the seventh tee for water. The starter and I tell him he can't do that. A ball could hit him. Concussion, you know."

"Certainly. He's a strong, handsome fellow!"

"I don't think he understands. Of course, he's Russian."

"America is a melting pot."

"Queens, where my firehouse was, is twenty percent black, twenty percent Asian, twenty percent Spanish-speaking, and where are the whites?"

"Well, there is an influx of Russians in Forest Hills and Brighton Beach is the—"

"Doc! The Russians are right here for the last few years."

He handed out a banana and apple to an old lady who looked ready for a safari. Only her gray gloves and gray spiked shoes gave her away. She could have gone to an elegant restaurant in her madras Bermuda shorts.

"Number forty-four. On deck," broadcast from the starter's booth.

"That's me. Nice talking to you." I didn't leave a tip. I estimated this fireman packed in at least two thousand dollars a weekend from the snack bar. We should all be so lucky. He probably had two jobs his entire life. He did not need any help. If people didn't want to pay my high fees when I went into practice, it would be all right.

Two Australian women with the Bermuda-shorts-lady and I made up number forty-four foursome. We teed from the large red balls, which were farther up from the men's white and blue. I drove with my nine iron. All four balls grouped one hundred and twenty-five yards down the fairway. I did not mind playing with women. In fact I got much more short iron practice. We never had to wait until the foursome ahead was out of my range because I never used a long club.

The three ladies played well, being British country set from a Royal Golf Club in tea-growing south Sri Lanka. They would fly out of Kennedy Airport tomorrow. They certainly made me feel good. Impeccable manners. "Doctor," showing pride, they called me. Our four white golf balls always formed a string of white pearls on the fertile, groomed fairways—until the seventh tee.

I was drinking from the fountain. I had not been sick. The water had to be good. Not bad, as the counterman implied. I looked up to this awesome pile of buried solid waste. In Virginia Beach people called something like this, "Mount Trashmore."

In the narrow shadow of the mountain, the crew-cut soldier climbed sideways as I had three days ago. The sides of his Army boots dug into paper, plastic, and ground. His balance was perfect. His fingers never dropped to touch the side of the mountain. His

71

green uniform shirt did not wrinkle. His narrow waist maintained a slight golfer's bend as he easily went over the top. He must have climbed the Himalayas.

"Ladies, do you mind if I hit?"

My large, titanium, club-head struck so the ball would fly up and either onto or over the landfill. It would go over anyone on the near top. That girl needed help. That soldier knew it, too. Did I really need an excuse to go up there?

"It was a pleasure playing with you. I must leave you three lovely ladies." There was fidgeting and wonderment among the proper Brits.

What weapons do I have? I thought. I recalled grinding my umbrella point before I went into New York City by subway years ago. I remembered clubbing a mad rat in a drainage tunnel in a lateral water hazard at the Garden City Country Club. That was the weapon—a club—and, of course, diplomacy or bedside manner, which are part of a doctor. I needed courage.

Courage wrapped in nerve allowed me to look over the edge onto the cap. Where were the people? I was relieved. The top reminded me of a New Zealand pasture except for tin tubes with tin conical hats interrupting the landscape. The landfill was vented.

The sunbathing panel was gone. The land undulated, leaving mounds with breezes and hollows with circulating winds or concavities completely silent and still—a dunes phenomenon. A reporter or policeman in a helicopter would see an uninhabited dump. There were four people here now—three underground.

Did my second, intended stray ball go over the top? Two hundred more yards and I picked it up. I did not see my first ball. As I walked, a heavenly surreal feeling returned—vortexes of wind and then no wind high up returned, and then a view of the reed wetlands, inland waterways, a canal, an outer reef, and the vast blue Atlantic Ocean. I lingered on the south edge knowing someday this would be the best course of golf courses. I imagined instead a kiwi plantation growing succulent fruit, purifying the air. I did not see my first ball.

A pattern of pathways, like pressed down rabbit trails, connected particular vents.

I easily picked up an entire metal vent. It was a tube insert that had vertical cutouts between struts and a conical cover. I looked down the tube into the black landfill. If noxious and toxic gases were being released, I did not smell them. Of course you can't smell carbon monoxide.

My eyes caught another rattling unit rise and move to the side. It was where the girl had been. The Russian soldier jumped up and out of the manhole.

"*Zdravstvuyte*, hello."

"*Privet*, hello," I answered less formally. I pick languages up in emergency rooms.

"This way." His arm made a reverse C as in "Come."

What should I do? What would you do? My clubs would not fit down a shaft, much less have swing room within a dump. Quickly I put five golf balls into my leather glove, like a blackjack, and put this in my jacket.

"Doctor?

"Come," in Russian. "Ki Kam told me you are a doctor. You told him. He says you are too, an excellent hitter of the ball."

I followed the crew-cut hair down a strong narrow wood ladder until bleached clumpy sand compressed under my golf shoes. Was it sand? We were under the surface. Would there ever be more light?

"Come. Get on," in Russian.

I felt his shoulder to get behind him on a baby carriage base. I sat on wood and we were off, downhill, deeper, in a southwest direction. Black earth collected in the crew-cut hair ahead of me because I was not leaning forward enough, and tightly held him up. Black walls, black ceiling, and white ground sped by us. He steered with a survival knife in the ground. It served as a rudder. Light from south vent tunnels caused the white pathway to sparkle. Faster we rolled and at the end we went up a semicircular path and then back and then forth until we stopped. We were in a "View Room." The blue distant Atlantic Ocean could be seen to the southwest at the end of the dugout space.

The high black walls absorbed sound. It was quiet. Off the carriage we could stand. What an excavation! We were thirty feet from the top. We walked toward the source of light and air. Abruptly, the soldier sat down on the white stuff. I sat next to him. I smelled smoke.

"Ki Kam, Merc." He nodded toward them. They were outlined in the open blue view.

Merc, her beautiful head pedestaled through a black poncho, sat and stared without focus. She was withdrawing in pain, inside her own mind. Light reflected off her fluted plastic clothes.

Ki Kam looked like a fly. One wing was a flamethrower. The other was a portable respirator tank. Both adorned his back like wings angled from his scapulas. He stared at me through goggles. He was between Merc and us; a black bandanna covered his forehead and hair.

He intimidated me. I stared. My pupils dilated while I listened.

"I am Tycek," whispered the Russian by my side. He had picked white sand from the floor and handed it to me. "Here, taste."

"Salt! Not sand," I said, not taking my eyes off the black fly.

"*Da*, yes. Be careful. There is crushed, melted glass in here."

That explained the sparkle in the floor. I observed the three people, two in black, one in green. I felt alone. All were grave. I had seen my family this way when there was a problem. All were thinking to find an answer when not one person knew enough. They were serious and somber.

I had never been underground in a room that could be a sepulcher. Should I be praying? I did not move.

White sclera magnified under the Viet's goggles. Ki Kam had two creases in each eyelid. Stare at me—that is all he did. We were ten feet apart.

There was more than one problem here. I did not want any electric shock treatment. I grabbed my golf ball jack; I squeezed the leather wrist to get the finger end to flex. Was a volcano going to erupt?

Yes, but not as I thought. Ki Kam sprung up, pulled off the goggles, and released his vest and belt. The flame-thrower and oxygen tank clanked to the salt floor. He coughed and coughed. He turned and entered an alcove. From a discarded refrigerator he brought us respirators with tanks, thrown out by a local Coast Guard station. He told Tycek in French to have us put those on.

These were ours for our stay. Methane and carbon dioxide were all about. Dioxin and metalloid particulate matter could be inhaled.

His coughing stopped. Tuberculosis. He had to be tested. We will all get it this close.

"*Non*, no," he said sitting again close, in front of us, reading my mind. "*C'est*, it is, a mold allergy *peut-être*, possibly, a fungus pneumonia. I am hot. Can you help, Doctor?" I actually understood him. Ki Kam was educated.

Tycek spoke. "Colonel, we must talk. Let me explain to the doctor our problems. In America, medical practice is very advanced. Doctors are leaders, Comrade."

"*Oui*, yes, Lieutenant." Apparently they had come to an understanding during the last couple of days.

"Doc, Ki Kam manufactures munitions under the landfill at the south and east end, away from people, but near the water. He had been an expert in Vietnam in weapons production, tunnel construction, and underground living. He was responsible for saving the lives of two villages near the South China Sea's Gulf of Tonkin from United States bombardment. He built an underground city."

He continued. "I am a Soviet sapper, a tunnel expert, as he is. As a soldier-student, I was sent to Vietnam to study the history of tunnel construction and survival. The legend of Ki Kam is basic to our education. I am now on my way back to Russia from Lima,

Peru. I directed the tunnel construction through which the Special Forces and police liberated the Tupac Amaru hostages from the Japanese ambassador's compound. I have special leave directly from Boris Yeltsin, who is happy with the Chinese-Russian summit. I have tracked my childhood friend, Merc. We are to be married. I am so helpless. Her state is so sad."

He was hesitating with emotion. "I am staying here as a guest of the CIA, Central Intelligence Agency, and don't want them involved. They were not to take part in Peru."

Ki Kam knew CIA and directed, "Merc, *si'l vous plaît*, if you please." He meant we were getting off the subject.

"Yes. Merc came...." Tycek choked again. "Came to visit her mother and father who were living in Brooklyn to be with her brothers and to see America."

His glance toward her silhouette made her move. I knew the story was true.

"Her parents never had a vacation nor traveled outside Brighton Beach and the Brooklyn District Federal Courthouse. Merc's brothers were hoodlums in Moscow. In America, they thought they were free to be criminals. They were caught selling firearms to federal agents. Both are in the penitentiary. That is not a tragedy. What is so unfair is that Merc's father, who walked with a cane, was knocked down by a gang, beaten, and robbed on a Brooklyn street. Merc's mother, who was younger and stronger, was shot dead ... in cold blood ... because she kicked and spat, fought the punks. Merc's father died in the hospital, possibly more from loneliness and grief than from blows."

Three of us, seated in rock salt and glass, looked toward Merc. She turned her head to us and wiggled out of her black poncho. She was hot. Our heads went down.

"Look how it has affected her. She doesn't sleep. She barely eats, and when she does it's with trembling fingers. She is fortunate to have followed friends of her brothers here because Ki Kam has been protecting her—more from herself than anyone else. He may have fed her tunnel rat. He wrote a Vietcong booklet about gourmet foods underground."

"*Arrêt.* Stop." Ki Kam said.

He probably knew English. Ki Kam pulled a brown pharmacy container from his shirt and handed it to me. Duricef. Patient: Mrs. Francis Jones, Baldwin, New York.

"*Donney-vous ceux-ci a la mademoiselle?*"

"Are you giving these to the young lady?" I said. "*C'est un antibiotic* for skin. Boils. Staphylococcus."

" *Je comprends*, I understand," he said.

He was practicing preventive medicine. Sunbathing was good under these conditions. I had to get her out of here. These men meant so well. There had to be more history.

Ki Kam started talking in French—very fast. *"Ma fabrique*, factory, *est* shut down...."

"Arrêt, stop," I said. *"Lentement*, slowly."

Tycek took over. "I must show you landfill. It's a marvelous underground architectural phenomenon, as you say."

"To me, it is already. Why haven't you brought her to a local emergency room?"

"She will not let me get within twenty feet." Tycek moaned. "I ask her *'Kak dela,'* how are you doing? Russians answer in detail and at length, but I get no response. I am a very patient man, but get only screaming and gesticulations and Ki Kam interferes if I get closer."

His Russian accent did not hold him back. I interrupted.

"It's getting dark. I'll be back tomorrow. Ki Kam, I will check you tomorrow. I'll bring medicine for you and Merc. Are you leaving, Tycek?"

"Yes. My government host is already suspicious of my absence."

We stood up. Ki Kam bowed. We bowed and my golf balls and glove fell out of my golf jacket.

Merc plastered herself against the intense red of the setting sun. Her nude body undulated in dance across the head of lipstick. Her hair rocked and twisted to her hummed lullaby of death. To have love—affinity—people need not talk.

It took us a long time to crawl out a south vent in order to circumvent Merc. What a figure! Tycek kept looking. Thirty feet of ladders and we exited a different shaft. I picked up my clubs and went to my car. Tycek had a rental. The golf course was closed.

———————————

"Another clear day," said the counterman.

"Give me four bottles of water, four hamburgers with everything, four French fries, four apple tarts, one large potato chips."

"Gee. That's the same order the young Russian just left with."

"Cancel it. One container of orange juice with four plastic cups."

"All right. I saw you on Mount Solid yesterday. Here. Look through a slightly opened fist. Like this."

We looked over the trees and fairways through our curved fingers around one eye and saw Tycek. On this July day he carried food in a white plastic bag up the side of the mountain. He was clearly visible. The mind focuses better without peripheral input.

"No clubs today? What's going on? Ken wanted to know if you're opening an office."

"No. Thanks."

I put the orange juice in my black bag next to the stethoscope. Plastic bottles of pills rattled below it. I was off doing what you should not do—crossing greens, tees, and fairways to number seven.

On top of the trash mountain, I used a Del Monte steel can to hit the false vent pipe hard. It moved up and off. Tycek popped out with a finger in his ear. We smiled; we descended to the higher floor.

Where were they? We put the respirators on and turned the oxygen valves.

"Come," in Russian with the universal arm movement.

We sat on a long furniture mover's dolly and glided down a forty-degree grade. Elm panel boards covered the base of the tunnel to the very deep end. Construction workers had dumped lumber here years ago.

"Hold it."

"*Het*, no. I can't."

"We passed them on the right. They were playing games in a 'Playroom.'"

"*Ũoõpó*, good. We see what Ki Kam has done. Amazing. He has closed down developing weapons because of her. Maybe he knows the war has ended. Maybe he has problems with the government. Maybe it's his health."

Our cheeks were next to each other as we talked. Tycek kept pulling on a V rope to keep the dolly centered. Once we hit a mismatched seam of panels and fell on each other.

To the right were light and air tunnels, the size of a crawling man. Still, the smell, a foul odor, pungent and metallic, was entering our masks. Microorganisms work on the buried garbage and convert it back to dirt. Toxic gases are released.

"I felt liquid!"

"Do not touch. It is leachate. Snow and rain drain down through the garbage, along the bottom plastic to exit pipes."

We went right through the thick, black plastic barrier on the floor into another world. It was cool and clean. "*Palatá*, armory," he said. The walls were red clay, neatly carved out. We ended in an earthen chamber at least twenty feet square with work benches covered by frames of automatic weapons. Some were still in their investment molds before casting; some in mechanic finishing vises after being caste. We were in earth, under the northeast corner of the landfill.

We got off the dolly and hung it up on a spike like a winter sled.

"Come." Tycek was in his environment.

We crossed the "Assembly Room" and entered a small dugout where clear, plastic water pipes descended. I could see pure moving water. Ki Kam had hooked into the irrigation system of the golf course.

"Thirsty?"

Tycek grabbed the food bag and handed me a bottle of water. We chug-a-lugged and stopped walking at the "Chopping Room." Half the room was full of aluminum soda and beer cans, pie plates, yogurt tops, foil, bike parts, frying pans, pots, car parts—anything aluminum. The other half had a homogeneous pile of dime-size pieces of aluminum. Ki Kam mined the landfill.

We bent through openings that Ki Kam could run through.

"This is the 'Melting Room.' Notice the walls, ceiling, and floor are waterproof. If water touches molten aluminum, explosions occur."

Five rectangular steel trays—with burners under them— lined up to melt the small pieces of aluminum. Foot-controlled bellows forced air over the fire to keep the temperature at least one thousand, two hundred and twenty-one degrees Fahrenheit. Exhaust pipes exited the top of the landfill.

"Venturi," Tycek said in English.

"Does he use natural gas?" Maybe he tapped into Keyspan's gas distribution system as he did the lighting company's.

"Some, but not here. Natural gas, with its carbon hydrogen molecules, combined with chlorine forms hydrochloric acid. Later, I explain."

"What's this?" I asked, pointing to a pile of small ingots.

"Magnesium. Ki Kam mixes magnesium with that aluminum to form the weapon alloy. After filtering and fluxing, see here, he pores into these clamped steel molds right through these sprues along the barrel rim. He also uses invested wax patterns shaped like weapons, burns the patterns out of the investment, and centrifugally casts handguns. That is a fine art—ancient, but accurate.

"The molten alloy is cooled to harden, separated, and treated. In the assembly room he machines and/or etches and shines the guns. See the used batteries?"

So this was his "*Fabrique.*" I knew from chemistry that on the atomic chart, aluminum was number thirteen and magnesium twelve—less dense, lighter, and very machinable.

"Who gives him magnesium ingots? What about fuel?"

"No one. He is extraordinary. I show you."

Leave two men with common interests and anything can happen.

We moved at the same time making our masks more comfortable. I carried my black bag, and Tycek held the white plastic bag with food.

"Down this hall are at least two large excavations. They extend under the golf course. 'Off limits,' Ki Kam says. One is the 'Organic Fuel Room' where he makes acetylene from wetland and dump methane. 'Extremely dangerous.' If oxygen, air, or chlorine mixes with methane, 'Blow up.' But oxygen is needed to make acetylene, and he has a method. Methane is soluble in alcohol. He makes methanol—camper's fuel.

"The other is the 'Plastic Room,' where he melts thermoplastics such as plastic bottles. He makes stocks and handle grips for weapons. 'Very toxic,' Ki Kam says. 'No enter.'"

Tycek thought and continued, "He has to have a 'Chemical Room' to handle chlorine, hydrogen, and other inorganic processes. Don't ever mix sodium and water; a bright yellow explosive flash occurs."

"Come,"—that gesture again.

I followed. I should not be here. My patients were literally upstairs. At a crisis, their illnesses had been going on for weeks.

"Here."

We went up a hole through the black barrier that sealed us from leachate. It was like exiting into an escape hatch in a submarine. There was a monorail crossing above us.

"Pull," in Russian.

I pulled a rope that brought from a higher-level two horizontal car tires on golf balls to our exit hatch. What a rattle!

The lubricated golf balls surrounded the aluminum cast monorail in pans that attached to the tires. The sound was that of golf balls in an aluminum frying pan—rattling and unending. I shuddered.

Tycek was in his tire before I could move.

"Get on the tire."

Down we went sitting in black tires in a circular tunnel enjoying a lumpy ride.

"Wow! Where are we?"

"We are at the southeast corner where the magnesium comes from."

I followed Tycek. He rolled off his tire like a rifleman positioning into the prone position. I mimicked him. How come he did not crush the food as I did my black bag? We turned as if getting off a bed. Stiffly, we stood up in a trench.

The walls of the trench rose high up into the landfill. I felt I was in an archive, between isles of books. Instead, however, tubs, masons' cement mixing pans, trays, and wheelbarrows fit on either side.

"It's the 'Pizza Room.'" Tycek laughed.

I understood. These were trays with salt water evaporating in pizza–like ovens cut out on the sides of the rectangular trench.

"I see. Ki Kam evaporates water, leaving rock salt. He covers the floors in rooms and tunnels with common salt called halite. It's sodium chloride."

"Yes. It's his method of asepsis. Makes pleasant and dry '*proyezd*,' path. But that is at ninety percent evaporation. He removes the halite. At one hundred percent, magnesium chloride, magnesium sulfate, and potassium chloride salts precipitate in the dried bittern."

Tycek laughed again. "This man is worth his salt. American saying. *Het*? No?"

"But magnesium chloride is not ingots."

"Yes, but sea water is an unending source of magnesium. The dyked canal south of here has a higher water level. Sodium chloride and potassium chloride are both needed by man for food."

I recalled from school—inorganic chemistry—that magnesium is electropositive. Dried magnesium chloride salt in an electrolytic cell will deposit as pure magnesium and give off chlorine gas. Chlorine, electronegative, can be used to make hydrochloric acid or be passed through metal melts to remove inclusions such as undesirable sodium, which is electropositive like hydrogen.

"Ki Kam's a brilliant chemist."

"Yes. Also an engineer. Hanoi."

"What's that rustling noise?"

"Ki Kam sweeps the tunnels every day. He uses the flamethrower, on and off. Hear the swish? The vermin are being swept out the east end into the wetlands."

"We are at the south east end. Let's get out of here!"

"Don't worry. He knows we are here. He'll cut the rats off. The on and off noise may also be released compressed chemicals, like his pepper spray or his insecticides. He carries these tanks also on his back. Dead sentinel birds indicate the flamethrower should not be used—like gassed canary birds in coal mines. He loves corralling rats and snakes."

"Let's get going. Merc must be alone. I'm afraid of suicide."

We rapidly climbed to the top of the east end of the landfill. I was concerned about our oxygen. We entered a flat area where a child's shiny red wagon beckoned to take us into another tunnel. Rapidly we rode the red wagon downhill diagonally through the entire dump to the west end below the "View Room." We passed the white windows seen from the snack bar. I saw flashes of the cute golf course. Now I stared at burnt paper and singed corncobs among stratified garbage. We ended in the "Kitchen."

Ravenously, we ate on discarded furniture.

"Let's find Merc and Ki Kam," I said. Tycek had to lead me. These black subterranean rooms, vents, and tunnels formed a maze. I grabbed my bag. My jacket was now also black. "Should I put this respirator back on?"

"It's best."

His intelligent eyes showed care. His Russian face expressed expectation of finding Merc. He put his mask on momentarily.

A faint, feminine voice cried in the unknown distance. Tycek translated numbly. His body, in front of mine, never made another sound. I listened to the soothing repetitive rhythm.

> *Reach in and take it out, dear God.*
> *Where are you, God?*
> *Squeeze, the blood to flow.*
> *Reform the lives gone.*
> *Reach in and take it out, dear God.*
> *My heart has a hole.*

Tycek moved faster. We climbed the original shaft and exited. He must have felt the sorrow. We dropped our respirators and tanks of oxygen in the grass.

God had not abandoned Russia.

She sat on a box sunbathing nude—swaying and singing in the afternoon sun. Tycek respected her space. Her long brown hair had oils that reflected light.

Ki Kam stood preparing a barbecue picnic in the quietness of a depression surrounded by the green rim of a crown. Oddly, his white hair stood straight up and out, punk style, influenced by London nightlife and hair spray. We were isolated in the hollow from the people below and from anybody who dared climb the mountain of garbage.

Ki Kam used a piece of scrap wood to stir the charcoal. He was dressed in neat black pantaloons. His small eyes sparkled intelligently. He had a plum face.

Usually there is inherent conflict among different people. I did not feel or see any here. Ki Kam remarkably planned to have a Fourth of July picnic except for the fireworks.

Tycek and I walked to the fire.

"*Dorbrey dien*, Ki Kam," the lieutenant said to the colonel.

"*Mes enfants*, my children," Ki Kam reprimanded. "What is wrong with you two?" Ki Kam formed his words. "She needs rest, time, prayer, thinking well … good happy times. We have to teach her new ways, and how to work. There is hope. She cut the hole in the poncho for her head. Her hysteria is lessening. The sun will shine. Her life will be beautiful, as beautiful as she." He coughed a couple of times and spat. I studied the spittle, looking for blood caused by fungus balls—aspergillosis.

I knew his approach was not working because of the distance she put between us. She reacted abnormally—head down, coy, and then at times violently to Tycek. She had reactive depression, born from a genetic imprint that I had learned about from studies. Her eyes had shown hate when she flagellated her arms and anxiety, anger, and agitation. She had downright inappropriate behavior. She was in a prolonged psychotic episode. I thought of psychiatric rehabilitation. Ki Kam was right but now she needed medicine, tests, and therapy. She can't deal alone with her own depression.

Tycek was talking. "Merc must feel responsible for her parents deaths. My poor *pelmeny Sibersky,* dumpling filled with spicy meat."

Ki Kam responded. "She is a *matryoshka*, a series of hidden wood dolls," referring to her personalities.

Tycek looked her way. A black crow crossed the sky. He spoke caringly to her.

"*Kartofel*, French fries, Mercury?"

No response. He did not know whether to approach her or not. He felt her nudity.

"Doc. You are a great golfer. I have watched you play an entire round. Scratch, *Qui?* " Ki Kam coughed.

I didn't understand him completely when he galloped linguistically, but I knew he was talking about my *golfe.*

"*Scientific American* informs us the golf swing is the most complex and difficult movement to execute. Positron Emissions Tomogrophy scans show most of the brain lights up with neural activity, especially the cerebellum."

Again, I did not understand his French completely, but I listened to make rapport. Ki was happy as if he were to retire. He shook oil and condiments into an aluminum frying pan.

"Oh my God," I said under my breath. I looked at a coiled green and yellow snake about four feet long—in the pan!

He saw me stare and said, "You eat it like eel on Christmas Eve. I am going to grill it."

I understood '*sur le point de Noel....*' I had to make my point, in French. "Look, Ki Kam. Take this pill and put the rest in your pocket." I emphasized, "It's for your lung infection. You must get blood tests. Neutrophil counts. You must see a doctor."

"Thank you, Doctor." He took a bottle of water, the pill, and swallowed. His white porcupine hair moved up and down. He looked cooler.

"Now, Colonel, can you get Merc to take this orange juice? I'm dissolving the contents of a capsule in it."

Ki looked over to Merc. Tycek was getting close to her. Ki Kam grabbed the medicated orange juice and hustled over between them. She drank. Her broad tan nose lifted up as she swallowed. Her upturned breasts lifted. All of a sudden she looked at Tycek's chest. Ki Kam was upset. She raised a finger and pointed to the gold cross sparkling in the sun on Tycek's manly hair.

Tycek must have been happy with her for the first time in three days. Readily he took off the gold chain with Orthodox cross and held it against the blue sky. I saw a sparkle of life in her eyes. I felt better, too.

She grabbed it to hold against her breasts. She cried and sobbed and screamed and with a cat-like movement got up and went into another green hollow. I then saw only her forehead and hair.

All of us, I am sure, asked ourselves what we should do. I knew that in fifteen to twenty minutes the major tranquilizer would take effect and we could take her off the landfill peacefully.

"Let's eat," Ki Kam said walking back to the barbecue. "Thank you, Doctor. Let's see what happens."

Snake, potatoes, and vodka. I offered my orange juice. Tycek distributed potato chips. Ki Kam was happy, Tycek on edge, and I? Well it was like being in an emergency room before a catastrophe, except my clothes were filthy.

Ki Kam said, "I've closed up. Not as young and healthy as you young ones. City mafya will be mad, but it is a man-eat-man world."

Tycek turned. Merc was by the edge.

"Is that safe?" I said.

Merc pointed down the mountainside.

"She'll be seen," I said.

Ki Kam moved swiftly with the hot frying pan still in his hand.

Beautiful Merc pointed with her extended bare arm, leg, and toe, her head held back.

Tycek started to jog.

Within seconds, all three were looking down. Ki Kam threw the flying pan down the mountainside—the chartreuse snake slithering in the air. Tycek threw Merc over his shoulder as if she were a duffel bag. She screamed and struggled. Her blue eyes glistened with tears.

Ki Kam ran back and beyond me. His plum face never showed emotion. He belly flopped onto a skateboard and rode right into a mouse hole in a green hillock. Within ten seconds, a vent was knocked over, an OICW—Objective Individual Combat Weapon—appeared. The white hair and black-clothed body of a Vietcong went into action.

At the edge Ki Kam took a combat position and let go two blasts.

I ran over to look. Two burly bodies lay dead at the base of Mount Solid. Nine-millimeter pistols were askew in the rough grass beside them. Two more men ran for the pump house.

Ki Kam adjusted white and yellow buttons by his trigger. His laser fire control and sight system focused on the water house.

Bam! An explosion of HE, heavy explosive 20mm ammunition, killed the hoodlums. Ki Kam's military rifle amo can airburst around corners, in front of and behind walls, at laser-measured distances. The weapon sight has a little computer. The 20mm HE round has a computer chip built into the fuse. This was his personal two-barreled home protection gun.

"Bastards. No shame. The murderers.

"Doc," he coughed. "I am sorry we can't have nice day. They want my methods."

"Ridiculous, Ki Kam. Tell Tycek not to leave Merc out of his sight. I'm going down to call an ambulance."

Not bad, I thought, for never being in armed combat. I started to shake.

"We only have two ambulances," said the Meadowbrook Hospital dispatcher.

"I need three, each with two beds."

"Doc! Doc!" yelled the fireman by the phone. "The police already sent for the paramedics. I called when I heard gunfire. What the fuck is going on? I knew someone was living there. Was the trouble the gruff Russians?"

"Yes. They were killed playing golf."

He looked at me as if I were insane.

We ran to the end of the first fairway. A row of response people, golfers, and onlookers formed a gallery. Many were Koreans, Japanese, and Chinese. The snack bar man carried his red hatchet from under the counter. The magnified sun was setting to the west. A north-south asphalt road allowed me to see the sun set—a slicing of the red star from the bottom, layer by layer.

A police car with an open window emitted voices.

"Captain, we suspect people are in the dump. We see two bodies, and suspect more."

Two police people, one with a master's degree, another working on her doctorate, huddled in the comfort of their car. I read their credentials later in the newspaper.

"We are not going in there, Captain."

An auxiliary senior police car pulled its window down. Two old men spoke.

"Who's going in? We certainly aren't!"

The volunteer fire department with siren and bell and horn blasting pulled up behind the police.

"There are people with guns up there," said the counterman with the hatchet. The new firemen held back and stood in amazement.

I waited impatiently for the ambulances. I expected at least five. I have to get her off the landfill. How were my friends?

The water department truck came. A drop in water pressure had indicated a leak.

"You can't go in there," said the policeman from his car. "Captain, Captain, we'll need a Special Weapons Attack Team. Bring the precinct infrared scope. The sun is almost gone."

The graded hum of the fire truck engines and generators deadened any nearby conversation. Their lights still rotated.

Finally I heard the ambulances with their wailing sirens. Their rear doors flew open. Paramedics jumped out, ready to go.

The neat policeman and spotless policewoman got out of their car. They were holding crime scene yellow tape. They talked to the paramedics.

"No one moves until we deem the area safe."

Talking to the police would be futile now. Civilian patrol cars rolled up. Pedestrians gathered around. Then I saw tall Ken's head above a Spills and Pollution car.

"Ken," I asked. "Do you want to help?" I thought, *Do you want to do something good, unselfish?*

He didn't answer. He was probably trying to word how much money would he get for it.

Then a civilian patrolman walked up to us. Ken knew him and introduced us. "Mr. Friedman, this is Doc."

"A doctor? You va young." He shook my hand. Numbers in black ink showed on the inside of his left forearm.

"Yes. Look. I need to rescue a girl from the mountain. Will you help me carry a stretcher and a rescue bag around and up the slope?"

"Sure."

It was as simple as that. Under pressure, there is always someone to help. Just ask.

"Follow me."

I took the stretcher and bag with intravenous solutions, tubes, and needles from the open ambulance.

Friedman was quiet. His compact, strong figure held up his end of the stretcher. We went around the tape to the west end of the dump by the road. He was more experienced than I, probably a survivor from Dachau or Auschwitz or Buchenwald.

No one was near. I took a flashlight out of the emergency bag. Friedman had his own.

At the top, I ran around rapping the vents that were now squashed down into their larger pipes. "Tycek!" I yelled. "Tycek! Ki Kam!" Friedman watched me. He went to the edge. I heard the hum of people escalate. A searchlight went over our heads.

"Tycek!" Again I yelled. "Tycek! Oh! There you are. How is Merc?"

"She's sleeping."

I had given her a psychotropic drug. She had to be exhausted.

"Bring her up. There are no more Russians. We have to get her to the hospital." Friedman looked down the shaft with his flashlight.

Slowly Tycek carried her up the shaft, never once letting her head touch the side.

Friedman and I took Merc's plastic-wrapped body from Tycek's shoulder and placed her on the stretcher. I took her pulse. Fine. I would not need the I.V. or the emergency bag of medicine. She breathed comfortably.

Tycek hit the vent pipe with a resounding signal that meant the same as milk poured into the water strainer of the pump house by the Mafya. The Russians, who had been coming to buy arms for some time, and Tycek, now, were saying, "I've come; there has been an exchange. I'm leaving. Goodbye, Ki Kam."

Tycek followed us but swiftly took the lead within our flashlights down the west end into darkness.

The ambulance people met us slightly angry, but were helpful after I told them I was a doctor and they saw Friedman.

They put the I.V. in her. A routine port was opened. Dextrose and saline nourished her. I turned away from the ambulance doors because a minor explosion erupted from the dump. The hum of people got louder. Police search lights sought Trash Mountain. I looked around. People where arriving in droves.

Tycek was talking to an impeccably dressed Euro-American. Black jackets with the initials A.T.F. written on the back moved about. F.B.I. jackets were worn as if on manikins. A S.W.A.T. team dispersed to positions.

Now, everyone stopped. No one moved. Only quietness prevailed after another igniting explosion—Firedamp.

"Move back! Move back, everybody!" ordered the police.

They didn't.

Another explosion and then all the vent pipes flew into the sky. Geysers of white flames followed. Red and white flames also came out the windows. The landfill shook and expanded outward. Areas of the sides and top imploded. The earth under our feet vibrated. Yellow flashes blinded us. A plume of gas asphyxiated us. People went to their knees.

Ki Kam had ignited the tunnels full of locked-in flammable methane. He detonated whatever chemicals, ammunitions, and arms he had in *La Fabrique*. Where was he? Land contouring for the expanded golf course unexpectedly started.

I faced the ambulance. Friedman was taking in the facts. Tycek came to my side. We shared knowledge. His crew cut was full of soot. I was black from top to bottom. At last, Merc had a clean white sheet over her. Friedman still had not learned of the four bodies, maybe five, out there in the war zone.

"My *pelmeny Sibersky*, my dumpling filled with spicy meat," Tycek muttered by my side while staring into the back of the ambulance.

"*Zaidi I Poprobui*, Come and try." I heard her. I actually knew what it meant. It is the story of love.

Tycek jumped into the back.

"All right, let's go!" said the paramedic.

The strobe light flashed. The siren whined.

I felt at a loss. Would I ever see them again?

I thanked Friedman. He was unassuming. I walked among the people; some still held their golf bags. The mountain was an inferno. A helicopter searched with lights and infra red equipment for a man thought to have lived there. The counterman told people he knew the country was changing.

I had parked my car by the snack bar near the first tee—by the practice putting green. It would not be blocked in and I could get back to North Shore Hospital.

In the parking lot, I put my black doctor's bag down to search for my car keys. Instead, I pulled out of my pocket a golf ball with a red dot. I had not played golf today. The ball had in red print "Dr. Jeffrey Taylor, M.D."

You and I know now. He was a prankster. He had a sense of humor. He was a smart nut.

With deft hands and a subdued cough he had among the high percentage of Asian onlookers said goodbye by putting the ball in my pocket. The Long Island Railroad to New York City and then to a *Québec* experience crossed my mind as his escape route.

It has been a hell of a Fourth of July! □

Redemption

Characters

Paris Newcombe
The Blue Gargoyle - Policeman one
Policemen two and three
Mrs. Peach Newcombe - Peachy
Mr. Newcombe
Principal
Coach
Eddy - The executor
Mrs. O'Hara
Charrise
Uncle Zacharias - Zack
Sugar
Buck Henry
The Pickanniny - Peewee

Time
Late nineteen forties and the millennium.

_____

The convention-like roar of New York City basketball fans exploded in his stentorian vision. Long-fingered black hands from defined arms defended. Excited people in the bleacher seats stood and pumped arms. Cheerleaders, the band, flag and banner holding students watched and screamed deafening praise and celebration. Sweating elbows and beige palms of defeated warriors dropped. Open mouths closed. Lips of the loosing players drooped as Paris Newcombe hit the winning jump shot at the sound of the buzzer.

He—a six-foot-four-inch growing teenager—stood on the winner's platform to receive his Downstate medal. Paris had a happy long face with demure, penetrating black eyes. He accepted the gold medal from an opened box lined with white felt. To no one's surprise, officials detained him at the podium to receive another—the most valuable player of the game award.

There was a shyness and efficiency to his demeanor. His work finished, he wanted to go home. He looked back to the nine other players, and to his coach and high school principal. He shared by nodding and smiled in gratitude.

After midnight, he lay stomach down on a bench at the L-shaped Queens bus terminal. One of his feet was in a shined leather shoe and it extended two feet beyond the bench. The other shoe supported his leg under the calf muscle. He laid his head and black curly hair on his right forearm. His left hand hung out over the side of the seat to protect his satchel. He awaited the final one a.m. bus. His nose breathed city air from a slot in the wood seat.

The visions of him propelling his strong, athletic body high above the teams' players, of the high bolted arena ceiling closing down above his head, the fans' deafening roar, the magnified sight of the netted hoop and the surrealistic whip of the net replayed in his adrenalin-stimulated memory. Dreamy clouds of the victory and the late dinner shuffled to replace each other as he almost fell asleep waiting to go home.

The pompous principal had praised him at the post game dinner. The stodgy man toasted the team and mentioned a new school sports plan. He venerated patience and perseverance.

Smoking a cigar, the coach exuded the all-knowing look of a father-friend who had the players under his control. In jest, he gave cigars and money to the players especially those who were poor. He knew this intelligent team could win the state championship. He merely said, "Nice job," and to the relief of the principal, "Upstate, here we come. Practice is after school, Monday, three o'clock sharp. You're free this weekend. Good work."

Clouds full of Paris' startling dreams shuffled in the space of light sleep. Paris' left fingertips drooped beyond his athletic satchel onto the cement of the bus terminal walk. Green clouds, full of the season's playing teams swayed back and forth. *Let's go.*

Cover that man. Follow your shot. Don't dribble. Shoot. Penetrate.
Lay up. Reverse lay up. Pass. Look for the open man. Hook. Hook.
Slam-dunk.

Practice had made him an accurate shooter. A black cloud appeared. It carried his talking, religious mother—a beautiful soft, supple woman with full cheekbones and tensor lips. Then another black cloud floated with his guiding, quiet father, who said, "Finish your shot. Follow through."

A big yellow cloud! He and his father, playing one-on-one in the evening behind the school in a yard surrounded by a green grass field and a cinder track, crowded the black clouds upward. He smiled. He loved his supportive parents, but they missed the victory. He felt alone. Not only had the coach left him at the empty terminal, but also he couldn't share the victorious evening with his parents.

Wakeful thought and feeling cleared the cumulus cloud sky of light sleep. Paris tried to supplant the hardness of the bench with the softness of a stratus cloud to lie upon, to rest, and await the bus. The ability to transcend the apparent, to alter reality, to endure hardship, to ride the white cloud of victory is the mettle of champions. He and his parents knew this, each differently. They perceived truth alike. Harmony resulted. Love smoothed the soul.

"Whack!" resounded from the leather sole of his shoe up his long leg to his alerted eyes. The sound and pain radiated to cement, to black parking places, to the depth of the moonlit night. Sound and pain ascended to the light from an overhanging portico and back down to the gargoyle face of a uniform policeman. The officer struck lightly his own left gloved hand with the nightstick. The leather thong of the billy wrapped tightly around his right white glove.

Paris with swiftness the policeman did not expect pulled his legs up to his midsection and sat up. He looked sideways and saw the puffy white jowls of the night-beat patrolman. The face was soft—of a man not in proper physical shape or weight. It was a devious and bored face full of blackheads—a waterfront face— one that wanted confrontation. The large eyes bulged.

"No sleeping on the bench!"

"Sorry. The bus will be here any minute."

"No drinking."

"I don't drink."

The foot swelled. Paris could only put weight on one foot, even sitting down. Pain made his eyelids flutter.

"Stand up."

Paris hesitated.

"Stand up!" The policeman butted the club into his left ribs.

Paris felt anger. He thought the demand was unreasonable. His eyes enlarged. He heard his mother's voice say the worst evil in life is another person. He tried to stand by putting weight on his left arm and one foot, but the nightstick undermined his arm and he fell down.

"I said get up."

Peachy, his mother, never talked in terms of black and white, but Paris intrinsically felt bigotry. This man came from another culture.

The officer was impatient.

Paris wondered why he was being ordered to stand up. It wasn't the time to ask for a time out. He envisioned putting his foot into a pot of ice water, which helps anesthetize swollen ankles, and felt the cold numbness. He was able to stand.

"You're a tall black bugger."

Paris smiled and looked down at the Irish troll.

"Get that coy look off your face."

Paris hadn't learned the word "coy" and didn't know how to respond.

"Who do you think you are?"

You can't win when somebody says that.

"I'll show you."

"Whack!" and the collarbone that connects the chest to the shoulder, that allows the arm to sink jump shot after jump shot,

109

was broken. Paris' bashful look disappeared. Anger swelled up within him. Paris fell back on the seat involuntarily.

There is no place for forgiveness here. "I'll not allow you to abuse me." His church upbringing started to blur. He became confused.

"Oh, you won't, won't yer?"

"Whack!" The back of the bench splintered. Paris swung his hand with the satchel attached, and it glanced off the officer's face. Paris retracted the bag to ward off another blow. Within seconds a police car pulled up. Two more men beat him over prone and handcuffed him. They dragged him into the back of the car, whereupon they beat him more until they smelled his urine-soaked legs.

The police car sped off as the huge lighted bus rocked to the bench. Spots and dribble of blood below the grip of the isolated athletic bag resembled a Pollack painting.

"Dump him," said the driver cop.

"Na, let's bury him. Look, will yer, at this egg of an eye."

"Dump him," said the third policeman.

Paris imprinted their faces. From the floor, looking up, streetlights with tin hats on sides of wood telephone poles offered solace as they drove ten blocks. The cuffs were released and the third guy kicked and pushed Paris out the back into the gutter. Paris hit the curb and cut his head again. Blood pooled around his body. He lay lifeless on bluestone macadam next to paper cups, candy wrappers, twigs, and oil from leaking crankcases.

At sunrise, a black woman putting her garbage out ran over to him.

"I'll call der police."

"No. Please don't. Call my dad. Only my dad." He gave the phone number.

In the street she looked at the gold medal in the open box next to his jacket pocket. She felt his pain. How? Why? She stared at his body and swollen face. Smudges of chewing gum and car oil and horse manure surrounded him. How could someone survive such a loss of blood? She ran past an iron fence, up steps into a brown clapboard house. A morning mist ascended from the street. Trunks of trees and quiet houses seductively exposed themselves. It was Saturday morning. To her, it had to be a hit and run.

Fear, the emotion needed for survival, had drained from his shivering body. Silence with the energy of creation replaced the untoward experience. Paris' father and mother carried the medal, the clothes, and his disjointed, gangling body to a Hydramatic-shift Oldsmobile. They raced to a hospital. They said only essentials to each other, such as, "This will be expensive." Paris let them think it was a car accident, although he suspected his parents knew dirty play was involved. What was he doing ten blocks from the bus depot? Respect for each other allowed the known to exist without outward acknowledgement or more definition. His parents were patient.

"Hypothermia," said the resident. "Wrap him up. Five percent dextrose I.V., stat. Tighten a towel knot under his chin. Support his head. Hematocrit? Clear eyes."

"I'll make it," Paris mumbled from the gurney. No sense in hurrying now and missing something such as the gurgling from his throat. A nurse cleaned up a clot that started bleeding again.

"Radiology, anterior-posterior lung plate, and then the operating room. Tell me about your son. Rheumatic Heart Fever? Hemophilia?" And on the questions came. "Alcohol? Leprosy? Tuberculosis?

"Wake up anesthesiology," the resident ordered. "You'll intubate if he doesn't get here."

The nurses heightened their pace after a quiet night. Behind swinging doors, the parents felt helpless and feared the worse. The resident started percussing the side of Paris' ribs as they descended the hall.

There was air or blood in the pleural cavity. The doctor stuck an eighteen-gage needle between ribs. Air hissed out. The resident felt the collarbone depression, and then covered him again.

"His leg is broken," said an intern.

"X-ray everything," said the resident.

"I can't find a vein," said the intern. "Shock!"

"Do a femoral cut down. I'll be right there. Airway open? Suction. Pneumothorax."

"Yes, doctor."

"Trauma-alert stat! Get both attendants. Hurry!"

"I'll make it." Paris' mind absorbed the hustle. His teeth chatted.

"Phenobarbital 200 mg. I.V. Slowly," said the resident.

At practice the coach found out about the accident after missing his curly black-haired Adonis. Paris consistently arrived early in the gym. A phone call to Mrs. Newcombe, and the athletic office stank from white cigar smoke.

How could he get eighteen points out of the bench? Impossible. There goes the state championship. The principal may take up smoking, too. I'll have to take a look at Paris. He'll be lucky to finish his senior year.

"You were the last to see him," he recalled she had said.

"What can I say, Mrs. Newcombe?"

"You should have waited 'till he got on the bus."

"Mrs. Newcombe, we have athletic insurance. It should help."

"You mean, you're not guilty?"

"This is an unfortunate accident. I don't know what happened. We'll visit him tomorrow. I'm sorry, Mrs. Newcombe. My sympathy to Mr. Newcombe."

She had hung up.

On Tuesday afternoon the entire basketball team visited Paris. He couldn't say a word. His eyes blinked between white, face-wrapped bandages. His plastered leg hung in a pulley system suspended from the ceiling. He was on his side and a tube drained his chest. Pathetic. The sight made Eddy angry. Ed was the "gofer" for the team.

"Eddy," the coach said, "tell Paris to blink if he needs something. Check him out."

That's how Ed got close to Paris. He started with questions about his feet inquiring up to his head. "Does this part hurt? Should I tell the doctor?" They communicated. Paris blinked once for yes and twice for no. It got confusing if he had to change a no to a yes.

Eddy's job was to hand towels and water to the basketball players. He cut the oranges into quarters for their sustenance. He couldn't make the team, but he could play. Wednesday the coach said, "Eddy, get out on the floor. Work your butt off. You're taking Paris' spot."

At the hospital a month later, Ed visited Paris for the umpteenth time. Paris knew the team had lost the state championship, but his eyebrows went up, not only in amazement, but also in a "Good for you" nod when Ed told him he scored two points. Ed told Paris there were high schools with nearly the entire school on the team and that their team was just not big enough. Of course he told him that if Paris were there, they would have won. Ed made Paris sad and regretted for the rest of his life having been outright honest and indirectly bringing up the accident. Paris' eyes watered.

These visits started a friendship. Ed knew Paris' immediate family, his house, his silence, and his recovery. He knew his career because he worked for him in his professional life at Paris' request. In later years, Ed was his secretary and now, some fifty years later, Ed was the executor of Paris' last will and testament.

Except for the three policemen, what really happened at the bus terminal no one knew. As executor, Ed had to make the decision to tell or not to tell the story if anyone *should* know—if there were an inquiry. Society is litigious fifty years later. People don't accept injury and heal. They actually go out and injure themselves and sue. So Eddy, who scored a high of twelve points in his third year of high school, had been very happy to see curly-hair Paris in the bleachers standing at a slight tilt.

Now, after Paris' death, Eddy wanted him to stand tall and straight like the great leader he had become. As Ed initially read the last will and testament at Paris' office desk, Paris' wife, dressed in black carrying her ever-present parasol, made funeral and burial arrangements. Number four of the will directives made Ed stop to grasp the financial picture of the estate because it read, "Give Mrs. Elizabeth O'Hara and her two children per capita one hundred thousand dollars. She lives at the following address."

Many thoughts went through the executor's head. In the forefront was an affair, which also brought up the question of what to omit or say at a reading of the will and to consider the justification and propriety of such generosity. Yes, some wills are available before the burial. All are not sealed with wax.

The answer to who Mrs. O'Hara was, and why Eddy eventually gave her children the money anonymously, flowed from the ancient event at the Green Bus Line Terminal. The truth emerged in an addendum, not a codicil, which was several typewritten pages of information stapled to Paris' last will and testament.

Paris suffered all his life. He hid his actions after the beating. It took him time to unravel many complex feelings and to understand that an act does not stand alone. Ed deduced this and detached the addendum because the pages were not the essence of the will, only an explanation. As executor, he didn't want any liability suits brought against the estate. He would have to defend them, and lawyers would drain the estate to the extent the family could be worse off; and he knew, as he read, that the estate, the family, would lose.

Eddy recalled.

Paris, seventeen years of age, had been released from the hospital with crutches and a beaten soul. He planned to study and understand what happened to him, and he determined to do something so it wouldn't happen again—to anyone. He needed extra long crutches, but he was lucky the epiphysis of his long bone was not damaged because his legs were still growing. Otherwise, one leg would have been shorter than the other.

Eddy knew more than the addendum explained. Paris had graduated from high school with a slant to his shoulder and hips. Arm, shoulder, and leg casts had pulled him down. It was hard to get him to smile when Eddy took a graduation picture, but Paris forced a smile for him. Paris took a year off after high school not knowing if his scholastic path was right and whether the college still wanted him.

He would sit in a comfortable armchair in front of a new television watching westerns. His mother and father were the first people to buy a television in their neighborhood. It was a Sylvania—better than the one with a magnifying screen, an RCA. Ed came over to tell him how the team was doing. Paris already knew. He seemed to know a lot. He showed Ed how to eye up the basket hoop over the edge of the ball. They used leather balls then.

Ed knew Paris had had many thoughts. It was confirmed as he read the addendum. He had wondered all his life why Paris had cut up basketballs.

It was unfair. It was not right. Any blow with the intent to subdue, to master, to enslave, to emit power, to be sadistic was a blatant foul. The three officers were hoodlums. They were oppressive, willful, evil people. There had to be other victims.

In the living room Paris said, "Momma, look at this article in the Press. The city finds about one hundred police officers a year that are unworthy of wearing the badge."

"Why are you reading that stuff?"

"Mom, there is a silent code, a blue wall of silence, in the police force. Do you think corruption will be found out and corrected?"

"Certainly. Look at Joe down the block. He is going into the PCCI unit—Internal Affairs."

"He is doing it for security. He can go either way. He hides his faults."

"Then the children must be brought up to know right from wrong."

"You're right, Mom, but it's a great burden. Ultimately young-ones have to want to learn right from wrong ... to incorporate values themselves."

"And Paris," she said dusting the living room, "there are people who know it all, who will not listen, who are thick-headed and ... young man, don't you get any ideas!"

Momma was right. Paris also talked to Eddy, but superficially. As Paris restored his strength, he devised plans, because executing justice was new to him. It was more complex than digging in to recoup, to fight back, and determinedly sink a basket. The aspect of inflicting severe pain and suffering, even death, preoccupied him.

"Mom, do you think Dad would mind if I visited Uncle Zack for a change?"

"My brother is a rugged troublemaker. He's the wild one in the family. Hunting, shooting, killing, skinning—that's all he does. Cooking and playing music are his only civil behaviors."

"He is warm-hearted. Maybe the heat and moisture of South Carolina will take the pain away from my bones."

"Your father won't mind, but be ready for a preparation lecture and protect yourself from mosquitoes. They carry fever diseases."

That summer night, Paris' dad said, "Take the clarinet. Zack likes the sax and maybe music will uplift your spirit." This suited Paris' strategy. There wasn't a lecture.

On the cold at night, rickety train, Paris tried to understand a fearsome aspect of life. His parents brought him up to respect law and order. Police brutality is a major way of getting information, confessions, even controlling behavior. Threats of all sorts are played back upon the alleged criminal. Prosecuting attorneys and the defense lawyers make deals. The differences between the sides blend. The ratio of bad to good remains the same. No one ever fooled around with Uncle Zack, or it seemed that way. Power makes right. Ultimately it ends some problems or issues, but it can bring up new problems. Power can even backfire.

The gargoyle cop always seemed to be looking sideways in Paris' recollection. The white eyes of the gargoyle stared at him. The man will never outgrow his bullyness, Paris thought. He never outgrew a culture of hatred. He did not believed in the sanctity of life. The three blue men would never be sanctioned because they act in darkness. They support each other. They strike; they analyze weakness and hit; they steal and boastfully flee; they avoid the strong; they case and decide the probability of success—all below the table of their badges.

Paris seethed. He had to retreat from the enemy. He didn't want to. It was the strategic plan. He could never forget.

The train whistle blew at a crossing. "Charleston," the conductor called out. Some thirty odd hours of analysis and plans of revenge stopped. Uncle Zack might have some ideas. Paris needed someone to talk to—someone distant.

The black 1939 Buick with a straight eight-cylinder engine waited close to the dust-covered crushed stone under the single lane railway track. Peachy, Zack's sister and Paris' mother, had written that Paris was burdened, hurt, and suffering in the mind. Zack removed his fedora and wiped the inside band with his handkerchief. *I'll just make the kid feel as much at home as I can.* He fanned his long face as he leaned back on the black metal fender. He put his left, white and brown shoe on the running board. Air passed between his tall legs.

The clog, grind, and screech of the locomotive wheels caused him to stare into the steel undercarriage and observe the slowing, reciprocating drivers and pistons. Startling expresses of steam and air from the Westinghouse air brakes hissed. Two train cars back, long legs stepped down, turned, and carried a black instrument case and a brown and white valise.

"Nephew, you look like me t'irdy years or so ago."

"Uncle Zack, you as dapper as Momma sezs. Beautiful car."

They hugged, smiled, and shook hands while admiring the similarity between their physiques. Zack weighed forty pounds more, but his overalls came up to his chest where a suit jacket hid his weight. Two car doors were open; so was the bumped-out trunk. They closed these. In the car they opened the windows to appreciate the coming wind. Zack left a stream of dust as they passed white men's plantations along the Ashley River.

Mom had said Uncle Zack made money smuggling booze. They were low country folk, from near the ocean. Zack had carried a flask in his back pocket and young Peachy cooked she-crab soup for the family.

Thirty miles out of town, the car screeched to a stop. The car body shifted and shook on the shock-absorbing leaf springs. Dust came from behind the car. From the high front cloth seat, they looked out the partitioned windshield.

A black parasol spun up and down playfully along the tops of fall crops and then emerged in front of the car's hood emblem.

Paris looked at Zack. A smile crossed his uncle's big lips. Ahead a young girl showing a bountiful smile with perfect white teeth crossed to the left front side. High-heeled black shoes, bigger than her feet, made the passage slow and deliberate—practice-like. Every curve of her teen body pulled against the cloth buttons that lined straight down her straining seams. Two hands spun the parasol. Paris's eyes never left her every imaginable part.

Through the left window, Zack began talking. The men exchanged a slow deliberate admiration for a slow coquettish, yet strong banter that Paris never forgot and had to have more of.

"A storm is coming, little Tuna."

"Bare feet 'ill get me home."

"Sugar still as beautiful as ever?"

"Momma's hooked up now, Zacharias. You're not to inquire anymore."

"Tuna, t'is is my nephew from Long Island. You certainly are a site to behold in te shade of t'at parasol."

"My pleasure." Paris leaned over Zack.

"My name is Charrise. All woman are 'Tuna' to Zack."

"My, young lady, hold dat tongue. Come over wit Sugar near soon. Bring Buck Henry wit you. Tell him we got roots to blow."

"You wouldn't be a northern agitator?" Her face peered into the door window.

Paris said, "No, Charrise. Getten away. Visiten. But I do have faith in racial justice. We had it up north."

"Agitator, little Tuna? You just come around and see what Peachy made here. He may do you fine someday."

123

Charrise spoke. "Zack, Henry says you're a money man, but won't support the Jaycees or Rotary."

"Henry's ahead his time. Tere's always violence, Tuna. He's right. If we work togeter wit less segregation t'ere'll be less bluster, but Peacon Baby, factory owners want cheap labor. Don't mind yourself. If we stick togeter we can make t'e upland area prosperous."

"But that's just reverse. It's sticking together … that's segregation."

"No Honey'melon, it's just family."

"Are you certain? Henry told Momma you're making a fortune in lumber."

"Only temporary. Truck farming. Dat's my future. I am to be a clodbuster."

She stepped back and looked coyly down and up. "You still liken Sugar?"

"Always baby, till te day I die."

"Maybe we come up."

"Sweets," Zack said tipping his fedora.

"My pleasure," Paris said as both men suffered to take their lustful eyes away from her glistening eyes, pearly teeth, and solid body.

They rolled first, and then resumed the rear dust cloud as they passed wildflower fields. The dust plume decreased as they entered live oak forests with some pine and black willow trees. Grass, leaves, and pine needles covered the road. Swamp water wasn't far below. Cypress and Tupelo gum trees laden with Spanish moss eventually shaded a river road that led to an entrance on higher land.

Red brick rectangular walls on each side of the maul road read "Sugar" to the left on white, painted wood and "Loaf" on the right. Peachy had said Uncle lived at Sugarloaf. Paris thought it was a town, but it was a hideaway in the Four Holes Swamp inland area where the visible neighbors were hunting and fishing clubs, lumber companies, or entrepreneurs like Uncle Zack.

"Every time I pass Sugar's place, I feel I'm running away from what I want most. I'm not sure what it is. Do you know what I am talking about, Paris?"

"Maybe."

"Henry's a stud. I like him. But now I'm into comparisons. On my side, I don't stop. Could Sugar have kept up?"

"That I understand."

"You need passion. Sugar liked tat. My passion goes on. It's not limited. Henry has one passion. It's hunting. I have many."

"You leave many people behind like that—if you go on, and it could be lonely," said Paris trying to stay awake.

"It is. It is."

125

A winding road with a bulldozed border berm on each side ascended to a cultivated field with a long red brick house, a couple of large sheds, and a stable in the distance. Paris felt the coolness of a water breeze from a river current on the opposite side of the house. Less mosquitoes and bugs passed the windshield.

The red brick house had space, like inside a church. The new cathedral ceiling displayed solid wood trusses and thick, one-piece wood crossbeams. The floor was dirt. "Loblolly pine, when I sharpen te saw blade. I stopped construction until t'e fields are cleared and seed sowed. Te wood is green. I have to keep te money comin'. You sleep here." Zack pointed thirty feet along the cement-block wall and foundation. A bed, set up on the dirt, had a mat of collapsed cardboard from a box next to it.

Paris put his valise, clarinet, and shoes down and crawled into the bed. It sunk. "Good night, Uncle Zack. I'll talk to you tomorrow."

In the night dream, mythical Henry and real Zack fought for the affections of Sugar. Blow after blow from logs struck each other in slow, winding, strokes. Suddenly Zack stopped and walked away leaving Henry gasping by the side of the river.

"Stupid," Zack said. "Why can't she have te both of us?"

And then a voice from an azalea bush said, "I like Zack; I like Paris." Wind lifted the speaker's black parasol and it went north to Queens, New York and Peachy picked it up from the back lawn. She brought it inside and baked with it open in the kitchen. A fire started in the oven. The pies turned black, the baking soda biscuits exploded, but Momma was in the sky flying a parasol to where she met Charrise.

"I like her too," Charrise said, handing camellias to Henry. Henry, with a rifle on his back, climbed Spanish moss and like Tarzan swung across the Edisto River and knocked on Zack's river door. The knock went "ca-plop, ca-plop." Paris woke up to the pumping action of Zack as he filled a double tub sink where they entered the house last night.

"You had an agitated sleep."

"I dreamed for the first time of people liking people. I burn inside and usually can't sleep."

"Whatever you do, you're welcome here and if you're up to it, I need a hand. You'll make money."

Both dunked their curly black hair into separate galvanized pails of water. That's when Paris saw his uncle had no tip to his tongue, and Paris associated this fact with Zack's speech. The "th" sounds of the words "this" and "those" and "them" were absent. A "t" or a "d" as in "Ted" replaced the "th" that the tongue usually forms as it strikes the edges of the upper teeth. "That" becomes "tat" or "dat." The tongue was sewed together like the end of a cut-off arm. He stared.

127

Zack perceived the visual concentration and said, "Shot off. Only part tat's short. Never seen so much blood, but tell me about you. Here. Sit."

Zack put out hot sugared tea and biscuits. Apples towered in a bowl.

"I was beaten like no man I know and the thugs will get away with it unless I do something."

"Peach says it was a car accident."

"You're the only one who will know. I must talk about it. It kills me that it was the law."

"T'e law?"

"The police." A grimace came to Paris' face.

"Te law can have te longest prevailing, expensive, backward effect unless it's changed." Zack didn't move. He just gazed at his nephew. Calmly, he continued, "When you see a wrong, you must stop it by force. If you can't, speak out about it."

"I want to. That's why I'm here. Force seems more effective than talk. Force seems to me the only way to get ordinary people to respond."

"What happened?"

Paris took off his shirt and showed him the dent in his collarbone and the scars over his body. Zack couldn't miss the shiny ingrown curve, carved on his forehead where he had hit the curb.

"I see why you haven't reported tis. Tere's no real justice in our legal system. It stinks. T'e judges back the police—actually tey need t'em. Tey depend on tem. And when t'e police need te judges, it's payback time—t'e same for money contributen lawyers and politicos who fund t'e judges sitting on t'e bench in t'e first place. If a judge forwards an action t'at he can try to another judge, or passes one he should learn, for objectivity, tese can be refunds. It is easy to squash a motion or extend a trial. You can convert such behavior into money.

"Sure, you may win a default judgment, but ten see what you collect. Judges are treated like God. What t'ey say becomes t'e ultimate trut for lawyers. Hire a local lawyer and see.

"Lawyers can lose individual morality; tey can actually steal surreptitiously or blatantly from clients, contrary to the ultimate benefit of t'e client. T'e little man is lucky if a lawyer talks to him. A lawyer's excuse is dat all he can give a client is his knowledge. Knowledge should be free! We should all help each other."

Paris saw Zack squirm in his chair. Apparently Zack had had difficulty with the South Carolina justice system.

Zack said, "Te law can do so much more." He talked as if the justice system and the police were one. "Prosecutors can be unprepared pissers, Paris. What's on your mind?"

"Don't tell Momma or anyone."

Paris told of the horror, including his deferred entrance to the academy and how he still practiced essential physical maneuvers, even climbing rope. He felt the warm attention from Zack. He looked out a waterfront window and saw a white crushed oyster shell path leading down to a couple of canoes beside the river. Zack had to have trucked those seashells from the coast. Several red targets, mounted on piled flotsam and in the woods, could be seen.

"I toss and turn if I sleep. Usually I can't sleep. Trying is futile. I sweat. I can't concentrate enough to read. I try, but must reread. It's useless. It's a hell of a life. I hear voices saying 'Black bugger.' No one knows. It's like I don't exist."

"Horrible." Zack put out pecans and more hot sugared tea. He sat down again and looked at himself across the table. He and Paris had long faces with big lips and intent dark eyes. Their knees hit the underside of the table. "You need closure. We all see tings differently because we have different brains. Let's see if we can tink alike."

"Uncle Zack, I feel dead inside, as if I'm no one, as if I will not be remembered. The basketball team liked me; they honored me, but I'm a fantasy hero. Is it a family curse? I feel ready to go to war. I'm ready to die."

Zack saw the kid needed support for his ideas. First a comprehending ear and second, support of a plan of action. "Tose men were responsible. Day should take te blame. Tere is no curse on our family. We are all driven by our egos. We know when somet'ing is wrong. Creative people we are ... and resourceful. Tere are ways out of our doldrums. We take care of our children. We are not hooligans. We must survive against sometimes overwhelming unjust oppression."

Paris asked, "Is liberty without freedom better than no liberty at all? I walk freely, but am I free?"

"Yes. We fought for liberty. Forever, we must fight for freedom—if we want it."

The two men stared at each other. The justice system is responsible for upholding freedom. Paris had lost his innocence. The hatred wasn't in him. It reddened the twisted faces of the three policemen. Hatred divides. Determination to eliminate hatred swelled in his sweating mind. How?

"You are right, tose men will live wit impunity."

"What would you do, Uncle Zack?"

People came to and went from the farm. A week later Paris looked at Buck Henry. He stood straighter, thinner, and stronger than Uncle Zack. Henry had a raccoon haircut and a head like a wolf. He moved faster than Zack, as a younger man should. Had Sugar picked a young buck?

Paris thought Zack and Sugar were fortunate to have a close friend such as Henry. Paris thought the instability he detected resulted not so much from who slept with whom, but rather, from how long they would continue to sleep together and whether Henry would become a long-term friend to Sugar, as Zack had become.

Henry moved with alacrity among the sawed tree stumps. He planted the dynamite, lit the fuse, and ran back to the group, which included workers who seemed to be abandoned seamen or released convicts. Charrise and another young girl stood starry-eyed. A couple of women and children looked on from the stable. Sugar stood with Zack.

BAM! Dirt, wood, pulverized roots blew up into the air in a sudden explosion. After the settling, Henry ran back to the next stump, lit another red cylinder of absorbed nitroglycerin, ran back to the group, and POW!

Paris found the dirt-brown plumb-geyser, mesmerizing. It played on his mind. Charrise and her friend had relocated to the background. He wanted to talk with her. She would be a wild and independent woman some day. Certainly, she could handle a family.

Paris looked upon the flattened stumps and chip-filled earth as a battlefield only needing picking of the dead bodies—a cleaning up for fresh, different growth.

Zack said, "Let's take a break." Heat melted life. The sun was on its trek back to the Tropic of Capricorn.

A "break" to Zack meant drinks—Mint Juleps or Tennessee whiskey in tall glasses with lots of cold water—and a swim in a pool diverted from the river. Afterwards out came the rifles and handguns, and Henry and Zack went at their target shooting competition. Paris didn't know who was a better shot because all resonating cracks of fire always had an answering sound of a hit metal plate or can that were targets across the river from the white shell walk—outside the kitchen window. One marksmanship game required hitting a steel box on a vine. Initial impact started it swinging until it was missed.

They let Paris shoot saying only, "Watch for the blow back on the automatic pistol. The recall will take your flesh if you have your hand on the barrel."

That night, when everyone was gone or in the sheds, Zack, as tired as he was, taught his nephew the care and use of the automatic pistol. Zack stood and took combat positions. He supported the weapon hand with his other hand. He explained the sights. "Always have them vision clear." Paris pondered this. Zack loaded and unloaded the chamber. "Is it empty or full?" To Paris' surprise, Zack field stripped the weapon on a red oil-cloth, walked the dirt floor to the icebox, and said, "Treat all firearms as if t'ey are loaded. It's t'e empty gun tat kills. Now put tis one together. I'm going to sleep."

After several days Paris started to sleep earlier because the plan of action developed. He saw a way out of the quagmire. He saw a future developing. In the background a black parasol covered his soul, mothering it in a hard rightfully demanding way. Sexual, spiritual, and physical growth was to come.

Later during his visit to South Carolina, a poor, uneducated boy stood holding a quart bottle of warm milk across his naked chest. Paris opened the front door and saw the sun and stable yards in the distance.

"Thank you," Paris said, and returned to Zack who poured steaming grits—white corn mash—into blue china bowls. Paris removed the rubber band from around the wax-paper bottle top and poured warm milk over melting yellow butter. Zack turned potbelly-stove toast onto the sides of the bowls and started talking.

"You have learned to suffer. It's your advantage. Your plan is straight and simple."

"I am not sure yet."

"It's what did Lincoln in."

"That was crazy. I am not crazy."

"Work with Henry, today. He has an honorable discharge. He has been a mercenary in Africa and is a hell of a firearms expert."

"I thought so. He has a distinct military bearing when he is running or shooting."

"Right. It's all implicit, unconscious. Training does it."

Paris always slightly stunned by his uncle's talk—his striking vocabulary—waited open-eyed looking for more meaningful words from Zack.

"T'ink tactically. Have alternative escape routes. Keep your distance. Watch a man's hands. Don't underestimate a soldier's or a policeman's gut feelings. In fact, trust your own. Confidence based upon having solid knowledge and successful use of that knowledge, is right."

Paris listened and didn't want to pry into his uncle's past or present. He might be in the arms or explosive business, he surmised. A storage room had boxes with Tennessee Valley Authority stamped on them.

"Work with Buck Henry today. I have business in Summerville. Friends 'ill be arriving tomorrow. Have da woman folk in da shed make you and Henry some chitterlings and red eye gravy."

Activity and people mattered to Zack. Paris wanted the same, but the passion for life he had had was not restored. Paris learned a different lifestyle.

Henry had coon hair, stiff and back. It emphasized his face. His cheeks, nose, and teeth headed out. His bright squirrel-like eyes darted and stared.

Paris projected Henry could get up and down a varnished basketball court faster than any player in New York. He knelt next to Buck Henry watching him cut fuses longer for delayed ignition. It was Paris' time to light the dynamite fuse, run to Henry, and look back. Buck Henry made sure Paris' first stick of dynamite had a delayed fuse.

Paris practiced. Together they planted sticks under stumps, ignited them, and ran. Sometimes they banded the red sticks together with a blasting cap pushed between the nitroglycerin absorbing wads. They liked the higher dirt geysers. They used wood matchsticks. Neither smoked. Paris asked Henry what they'd do if they all don't explode. Who would go back?

"I've been there," Buck said.

They made progress, removing roots from the back land close to the oak tree forest. "Trees that could have been used in the hull of the Constitution," Henry said. The farmhands walked horses that pulled metal grates along the cleared land to elevate rocks and level moguls. Shortly the land was to be harrowed, plowed, and planted, and harrowed again to cover the seed.

"Liquid nitroglycerin is unstable. Watch."

One of the red sticks sweat. Buck Henry wiped off the liquid oozing out of the stick and threw his hand into space. A "crack" and "pop" from the small amount of nitroglycerin exploded in the air. Buck's squirrel eyes lingered on the explosion.

"Enough. Let's check the irrigation ditches on the cultivated land."

They stored the dynamite in a cool subterranean room.

They lifted a few water gates above ground and shoveled or hoed wherever they wanted faster water flow.

"Look, that's a Copperhead snake. Stay away from Eastern Cottonmouth crossing the river and swamp."

Paris followed Henry around the land doing what Zack initially had planned and conveyed.

"Can't wait for supper," Henry said.

"At sunset, the shed people will have dinner ready," responded Paris. "Let's take a swim."

"No need. Look at that thunderstorm a-comin'."

They ran to the main house with its cathedral ceiling to look out at the riverside for the downburst of air and rain that preceded the black anvil of clouds. Lightning struck devastatingly.

"In a few minutes we'll step out and wash."

With soap lather, they washed in the rain by the riverbed. The pure water—sometimes burning if a latent ice stone came down with it—felt good. After too many ice stones, Paris sat under a picnic table. Then Henry got under and said, "You're staying for Bobcat huntin'?"

"Let's see what happens. Uncle Zack wants me to bag a buck in velvet."

"Inside I'll give you help assembling the automatic pistol. Sometimes Zack just goes off leaving everything to us. If I go off, you know, the place is still here. If the folk go away, it's a wasteland."

The dark clouds blew over. The river rose. A cooler breeze brought a tremble to the land.

"That's a 'quake.' We're on a fault."

"Wow. No wonder the main house has thick walls and trusses and thick beams."

"More than that. Zack is handing out blue passes—just marked paper—to anyone who plays an instrument within sixty miles. Musicians 'ill be coming from Harleyville, Summerville,

Charleston, Waterboro, and even Holly Hill. Some woman comes, and it lasts all night."

Paris watched Buck Henry disassemble a Browning automatic weapon and then Henry put it together blindfolded in less than fifteen seconds.

"You don't want to lose the touch when you stand. You stand alone, a colored man." Buck showed Paris how to support a rifle and squeeze a trigger. "Strengthen that finger for a smooth pull."

Paris hit more targets using a rifle in place of the pistol. He had become more determined. He listened and changed and finally wanted to compete. Henry smiled at the thought.

Zack and Paris were getting up earlier every day, more together than apart. Zack talked as he cooked. "T'e justice system was intended to protect a status quo, to juggle t'e laws based upon reason. T'e present system was never intended to replace t'e natural law nor t'e spiritual laws of God—of t'e Bible. Laws represent t'e fair thinking of man, but laws are juggled when applied as if to meet a prevailing judicial consensus."

Uncle Zack saw the future. Paris saw him make the future. That was real power. Paris knew Zack needed better management for his passions and holdings. Would there be a loss of the freedom for which Zack had so intensively fought during every day of his life? Where was man's obligation? Labor or defend freedom? One thing about Zack, he gave a person undivided attention when someone was talking to him.

"Paris, tonight is my second annual music festival. Only people wit an indigo pass get in. You can help Henry at t'e Sugarloaf entrance. No whites, or else t'e old-timers will not feel comfortable. No children, or else mayhem. Only a musician guest of a blue pass holder can get in. Check t'e car trunks and t'e back of trucks for stowaways, or t'e farm will be trampled."

"How are you setting it up?"

"Te hands are setting up tables, chairs, and cots along t'e walls of the grand room. Put your bed along te side. Hide your belongings."

"How many do you expect?"

"Sixty."

Henry put a man in the hill with the Browning automatic weapon. A green Hudson came up.

"No young ladies, Sugar."

"Zack didn't say no."

"Only the kitchen then, for the girls. No running around the stables."

Paris misplaced his list and told Charrise he would talk to her later. It was the second time he saw Sugar, Charrise's mother, who protectively stared him down. Henry let the car pass. A tall instrument shaped bag had its head passing through the open back window.

Most of the musicians were serious and single. Henry had instructions to write down the names of people not invited. Paris did this while Henry explained that possibly next year these people would be invited. They had to practice and play at local jazz-sessions first. Usually the rejected players understood after talking of whom they knew and how they heard Zack's sax. But Henry did his job and they left peacefully.

Some traveled fast and far to get here and Paris changed flat tires and gave five-gallon tin cans of gas from up the farm to both guests and want-to-be guests. The scene by the red brick walls was an encampment. Small fires were lit. Music and singing started by the road. People huddled and held each other for warmth. Paper bags held food and people passed it out. They talked friendly—especially the Charlestonians—and Paris thought people needed more of this communal spirit up North. He felt badly keeping them out.

Henry had his hands full. More stable help, some of the tougher ones, came down while blue-pass-flat-beds went up to the house. Actually there were two festivals. There was nothing Henry wanted to do to stop the one at the entrance. Once his authority was established, Buck Henry let them be and sent Paris up the hill.

Paris walked through the parked cars and trucks near the long house. Men with hats and jackets quietly listened to the flat sevenths and thirds and tonal chords of the jazz. From inside through the many windows—all with shadow producing candles—rifts of rhythm and blues or rock guitar or mainly improvised chordal sounds emanated. The outsiders waited their turn to enter. Inside they would move sideways to the end of the house where they took their turn playing, pushing up the sound, adding and improvising to create a pleasant, new, even disrupting, yet accepted, feeling.

Paris saw the men wet their lips, blow their reeds, check their muted trumpets, put them back in their cases, bend over, sway with the sound, anticipate entry. Their sensitive ears searched for meaning. They could tell who was playing. If they couldn't, they soon would. Jam sessions were a world of their own.

Zack had just given a soprano saxophone solo and walked toward the open kitchen for water. It was a smaller sax and in the key of "C."

"Uncle Zack, here are the lists of people who had no pass."

"Put tem on t'e shelf above te ice. Move. You can take my place up front."

Paris looked at Charrise passing ice water, Hush Puppies, and moonshine whisky onto the table. He looked up and saw the little colored boy, who lived here, on a cross beam listening, looking, and enjoying his lofty seat. Smoke-swirls surrounded him.

Zack left Paris alone. Paris would have to step out of his preoccupation and come out as an integral person. This would be his decision, nobody else's. Peach said he played clarinet. He doesn't have to be the greatest, just my nephew. But this doesn't much matter. Musicians are tolerant. It had to be Paris who would want to sit in and jam.

Paris went to the space behind the water pump. He opened the clarinet case. He touched the straight line of keys, tested some mouthpieces, and assembled the woodwind. He passed by the musicians sitting and standing along the concrete block wall. He heard someone say, "Little Zack," as if they knew about him. People warmly looked up to him. "Sho'is."

People were tightening strings on guitars or basses. Some tested lips to shining horn mouthpieces. A new ensemble took its place at the end of the Great Room. Everyone had seen Paris before because he had collected the blue passes.

A small fire, all red embers, burned in the dirt of the living room floor. Zack had said he was planning for a spot to put the future fireplace. Now, the low fire opened the view for the listening musicians to watch the players and their spidery fingers or distorted movements. Mainly the players looked off into space and played implicitly. The sound was blues.

The pathos of blues brought a big singing woman to the musicians. Her words about life and the condemnation of past slavery and present sharecropping were repetitively sorrowful. The song approached gospel. Everyone listened; there was high tension. A trombone blew. She bellowed out:

> It's hard to be black in America.
> People can lift you up.
> The suppressive ways of the white,
> Get in your way, in your way.
> Don't take them on.
> Music is my master.
> Never let them bring you down, bring you down.
> Be one in the rhythm of life … life.

Men everywhere had hair on their faces—chin hair, lip hair, long eyebrows, and full beards—all enhancing glistening eyes. Some of the players strummed sorrowful, deep chords on their guitars to highlight the vibrant intensity of survival. Gold jewelry glittered on fingers and wrists in the light of candles. Faces lifted to the peak of the longhouse. Fingers slid up and down boards with clamoring repetitive alliteration—on instruments, some never seen by Paris.

Paris filed next to a flutist. Up came Sugar in an indigo-dyed scrim skirt, carrying a tall, double bass violin. Then a man with various sized cowbells on a standing wood beam came forward. He was a guest. Zack came back with the pipe-shaped saxophone. People nodded with approval. Improvisation started, which allowed tall Paris to fit in. Cigarettes flicked out into the room. The women and girls back in the kitchen stopped working. Sugar's violin sounds resonated rhythm, but clarinet and flute took over the melody. The patina of a pastoral pulled listener to rivers and mountains far from cypress swamps.

Listeners' arms went up and out; sides of hips slid suspended; Negress bodies slowly turned. Downed heads arose. Smiles livened the shadowed depth of the room. Melodic beats from hand-darkened drums, hallowed by muted bells, drew out the saxophone accompanied by banjo, ukulele, and clarinet. Attention stirred outside as soft beats, rhythms, and melodies resonated.

"Dancin'! Let's dance." People in parked cars came forward. Paris' clarinet pacified anger. He blew his own tune. He felt better. He saw patient communion among the country folk. Speed no more. Life is short. Close dance.

The poor black boy followed the man with the horse drawn plow down the turned furrow of raw earth. He looked at Paris' shoulders and broad sweating back—slung with the leather rein. Paris pitched to upright the winged wood-handle of the steel plow.

"Milk," he said, seeing Paris stagger to keep the blade from digging too deeply into the earth. No answer. He hugged the quart of milk to his bare chest. The sun baked the moisture out of the land.

"Milk?" Still no answer.

Paris concentrated. His body and muscles shook right and left. The workhorse went forward. "Stay out of te justice system," Uncle Zack had said. "Deal with honest folk. Be honest and tere won't be need. But don't let anyone take advantage of ya. Be a lawyer yourself. You can do it."

"Milk?" asked the Negro boy.

"Whoa," said Paris. He wrapped the leather reins. "Hi, Peewee. Thanks, Peewee."

The boy looked way up to him. Paris thought, *He's got to get school in him. He doesn't talk in sentences.*

"I have something for you, Peewee. Tell your mother you're going to spend tomorrow morning with me."

A quart of milk wasn't much to drink in this hot work. He wanted to walk to the barn, but kept working to the limit. The horse's water would come first. Farming was better than physical therapy.

Time passed fast. Buck offered to come up North and help clean up Paris' problems, whatever they were. Charrise, always ready to argue any subject, always smiled and let Paris know affection lay deep and it had to be nurtured. The work hands liked him and the woman gladly cooked pig's intestines for him. He refused hunting, though he liked eating venison. "Just don't want to do it, Henry," he said.

"Te few mont's have been special," Zack said. "You did real good. Here."

Zack gave money for two year's living expenses for Paris to return to school. Zack wasn't sure of Paris' plan. Neither was Paris.

Back home on Long Island, it was good to squeeze Peachy and shake his father's hand. It was Ed who didn't understand Paris' silence and lone behavior. "You certainly look terrific," Eddy told him.

Now, at Paris' desk, Ed mentally united what he knew with what he read in the will's addendum and in personal letters found among Paris' belongings. Ed read the following letter found in a pile of personal communication. It was a rough draft.

>*Dear Charrise,*

>*You are the only one who knows what is going on—that is, our ultimate destiny. Distance is painful.*

>*I have felt growing love for you. In you I have seen willingness to change; I have heard a desire to put into reality those ideas you know have to be incorporated or altered in a relationship. You certainly understood most of our discussions.*

>*You used selective reasoning to advance your wants. When we were out socially, you used selective meaning to advance your ideas.*

>*I have put much time and effort to see if real love can be elicited from you, and if you are able to see the normality of love and sex, and to see that together they are exquisitely complementary.*

>*Apparently, you have an agenda all your own—regardless of your mother's influence. You communicate extremely well, differently at different times, and recently very clearly, you wrote you're not interested in me physically. This is so much a part of male-female relations that it seems ridiculous to write letters any further and hope for special communication in a sexual way that doesn't exist.*

>*I must express these ideas, nothing you do not know, and take your advice, which I respect, appreciate, and seek. You say I*

must be temporarily satisfied with the beautiful feelings, emotions, and thoughts you have within you, not your appealing exterior. You're a Terrier.

If someone else came, she would see me as a human being, not merely a vehicle of sex or future money or a man to be controlled. I agree we must know each other better. You must be brave and understand a man. How many ways do you see me?

Affectionately,

Ed presently did not understand the confusing relationship, which still went on after Paris' death. Charrise's puzzling complexity lasted. He had heard some of their marital arguments. Now she was picking a casket for her husband. He had died from secondary hypertension, which can derive from kidney disease caused by primary high blood pressure.

Ed remembered Paris sitting to the roof in Peachy's car in 1948 and going to Queens, New York to investigate who the policemen were and where they lived, although Ed did not know it then. They had talked superficially as if Paris had more important things to do. He had wanted more old basketballs from the gym. The addendum and letters answered Ed's questions held from the nineteen forties up to the present. Charrise had to have been brave to marry Paris.

Outside in 1948, after midnight at the long, L shaped bus terminal, Paris bowled a reassembled "World Globe" between the shoveled mounds of snow down the length of the brick building. Covered by a layer of punctured plaster, the tin globe sounded like a spinning top coming to a stop.

It had been difficult to keep a leather basketball round by reinforcing the inside of the ball by crossing sticks of dynamite. He tried putty and glue. Inflation was incompatible with a burning fuse. Experimentation with ventilation holes, sewing balls whole, and taping balls, had been futile. So he customized a globe.

The strike of the match a few seconds earlier and the hiss of the lit fuse inside the tin globe lingered inside his head. The moon and portico lights gave him light to see the strike.

The Blue Gargoyle walked from around the shorter brick wall to the corner where his path and the longer path of the rolling "Globe" met. It was the corner at the end of the long overhang— the corner past the row of empty bus stops, past the splintered bench.

The policeman saw the attractive "Globe," and bent over. It exploded in his face, lifting him to smithereens!

"Dresden again. Newcombe kills O'Hara." Paris Newcombe slowly walked back to the borrowed car. A heavy automatic pistol caused perspiration against the indentation of his lower back. Extra magazine clips clicked in his jacket pocket.

He did not have to sprint. He felt confident, like a man should. Adrenalin caused his eyes to roam and to be ready to engage the other two men if they dared try to stop him. No one was to be seen. It was one a.m., February 1948. He was eighteen.

Back home, while his parents slept, Paris removed a dummy dressed in his clothing from the lounge chair next to the picture window. He turned the television off, closed the wood-slotted blinds, and sat in the armchair everyone knew was his. He felt satisfied that he didn't have to change clothing or hide his weapon. He had gotten away.

Even Ed—enticed by Paris's more attentive, less evasive and resolved demeanor—felt better. Mr. and Mrs. Newcombe felt a long hurricane had ended. Paris played basketball again, first with his father and Ed, and eventually with the best players in the city. He secured his position for September on the West Point team.

Some time after the gargoyle's death, two tough nervous men walked up to the front door. Peachy said her son wasn't home. She intuitively knew something was askew. No, they couldn't come in. She didn't care if they were policemen. She called the police. Five minutes later there were four, then six men outside, two from her local area in uniform.

A detective came to the door. "Nothing to be concerned about, mam'. We'll straighten this out at the precinct."

A few days later, Peach saw the automatic pistol while thoroughly cleaning a closet. "Where did you get this?" she asked Paris while he wrote a letter. "Is this one of Zack's?"

He stood. "Oh, yes, Mom. It's about time I bring it down to him. It shouldn't be in this house."

She stood under him, confrontational like. If there weren't love and respect and appreciation, this wouldn't happen. He knew it.

"You had better," she said, knowing her authority came from him this moment. She held her pride in him to herself.

Ed remembered missing Paris during the summer of 1948. He had assumed that Paris and Charrise had seriously cemented their relationship because two years later in 1950 Ed met a talented group of southerners at Paris' wedding. He never forgot a disheveled, miscast boy called Peewee, who in a short, nonfitting suit sounded clarinet as if he performed for Toscanini.

Colonel Ed's executive work started. In Chechnya, Russia relentlessly bombed people and homes. Money is redemption after bombing people and their country. Aggressors don't want to be complete failures. America, he thought does the same. Paris had to be freed from the life and afterlife bondage of sin.

The will and addendum were signed:

General Paris Newcombe, U.S. Army, Retired. □

Covert Americans and *Las Ramblas*

A filly nibbled on the Irish grass at the foot of a green hill. Creeks and rivers flowed from gray rock mountains. The farmed incline of the barrister's land leveled off into sand and sea. It was June and at water level below mountains and hills, Killeney Bay sparkled a silvery green.

Retired from the FBI, Tricia Poole tried to be happy replacing investigative assignments with hour after hour of practice with bow and arrows. Exhausted, she would jump onto her thrust-propelled Sea Doo XP, and speed east, on the darkening, ominous Irish Sea.

♀

It was 1998. "Ladies, are you satisfied? Another tea, water, or milk, and let's be off." Poole spoke out loud along the patio enriched with white wrought iron tables and chairs.

The Nná, women of the Pale, which is Dublin and its environs, were a select group. Half read the *Gay Community News.* They followed Poole to the side of the terraced patio onto the lawn toward a turbulent river. A handsome, athletic lot, they were determined to defeat the city of Cork now that Poole kept rank and added strength to Dublin's female archery team.

"Mabel, set most of the boys under the stone bridge. They are to count the arrows by the color of the feathers, and tell them to keep better order of the columns of numbers. I don't want bales of hay downstream this time. They could end up in England.

"Ladies, this afternoon boys upstream in the grazing fields will let loose bails of hay and we will be striking from three hundred feet with the long bow. Nine hundred feet is your goal. Let's prepare."

The woman lined up. An hour later, rainbows of arrows continued to pierce the cumulus clouds to rain upon the fast moving river and its floating targets. Some ladies, brushing against each other, aimed at bales of hay stuck on the riverbank or on a boulder in the middle of the river. They wanted to giggle, but such merriment seemed childish. A smile or a pat behind white shorts was sufficient recognition of a good shot.

"You'll not be cheatin' in Cork. The River Lee is wide, flat, and moving. Mabel, tell the boys to start yet another column headed Bank and Boulder. Are yer ladies joken me?" Poole said in brogue. She wanted to see who in the club was a lazy, wise arse. Cheaters held no respect for other people. She could conjure up enough respect for cheaters if they smartly got away with it.

"Lady Poole," Mabel said, "there is a message from Trinity College for yer. It's that there is a message for yer. Yer wooddin be kiddin me now?"

The sweat on Poole's forehead flowed slightly more profusely. She scrubbed her blonde hair and forehead vigorously with a towel and left the woman to relax, now that she was going to "boomin'" Dublin.

The ladies heard the motorcycle in the courtyard, and looked inquiringly and acceptingly at each other. She was Trish Poole. They felt secure and happy to have her on their side.

This woman is frustrated because she deals with men. She is attracted to men who are aware of their orientation and susceptibility to the power of sex and yet are not conquerable.

It is the dominance and the power over men that she wants—the expressive orgasmic control. Only then comes the peace—the tranquility she seeks. As ethereal as fighting is, she goes on to kill—energized and charged by the emotions of dominance and peace, she kills, she defends, she fights, she claws the demons of her mind and so, so completely fulfills the contract.

This description Owen put in the database. Poole was well suited. Owen had recommended her. Owen had known her for twenty years. He did not care what the Cardinal thought. The Cardinal possessed the intellect, but not the power of strategic planning, of world contacts, of decisions over life and death.

The Pope led; the Cardinal, also a given name, counseled and subtly influenced the entire business. Owen always considered the Cardinal and had to out think him, which was impossible. But all Owen's reports, all his insights were directed to the Pope, who held ultimate power.

The Pope held the position of curator at the university museum, but officiated the international killing business under trees, in corners of libraries, in bathrooms, reading rooms, and on the "Diag" of The University of Michigan. Owen, third in command, administrated and coordinated the business in which he aspired to lead. The Pope, old and wise, groomed him to become chairman. The future of the Cardinal, a professor of literature, would be worked out.

Why a business of murder? Why do this act—so heinous? If young, clean cut, enthusiastic cadets, see crime, drugs, and live in a world of fraud and are trained to strike against criminals, to apprehend them, to suspect everyone, they will enforce the law until a certain "calm" occurs—a period of self-evaluation with their possible transformation.

Federal agents may wish and desire the noblest of ideals. Some can dress neatly and walk with the mentality of nobility into crime, into excessive search and seizure, possible rigidity, eventually bias and limited observation, which are very hazardous to the normal, moderately informed, and caring citizen.

Megalomania floats to the surface of the controlling diabolical mind, like cream over coffee covering the good initial purpose of a supposedly lawful systematic way of life and thought, only to lose the warmth and kindness of humanity.

Owen had seen this among the righteous, the law enforcers, and the uniformed protectors. Eventually some become killers as he.

Owen settled into a university environment, in an office at a desk where he blew dense BBs through a short white straw. He blew from behind the computer, the cabinet, and turning fast and aiming, he emptied his lungs at a human target hanging on the back of the entrance door. These blowing actions—a habit he started in the fourth grade of grammar school—had developed into a deadly art. Here, at the university, he was undetected, unknown for what he was. He blended, losing identity among one hundred thousand people especially at a football game where his business was conducted.

He loved his wife and five daughters. If you love a daughter, you let her be, so she will search, explore, learn, and develop to her maximum potential. He lost his wife this way, by being too understanding of her desire for open marriage. She has since traveled one hundred and eighty degrees. Still loving her, he was insecure and searching for what was or what could be, in his red rubber heart.

He hated murderers. Truth comes hard because this fact opposed his persona.

He eliminated dictators, ruthless monarchs, perverted sheiks, and terrorist clerics. He should hate himself but he did not. Most money for his work he has never seen. Some passed to his ex-wife, his girls, and their education. The remainder of the money, in mountain cities and island banks, he only thought about. Numbers of accounts and keys were his only connection to it. All the money hoarded for retirement, will probably be left behind as a trail that the noble minded such as kings, queens, lords, monarchs, dictators, dukes, moguls have bequeathed for millennia—a track of coins covered by the blood of the oppressed, repressed—all beaten into subservience and controlled for self aggrandizement under the guise of the better order.

Owen's history was quiet. There exists no wars, no conquering soldiers or raped and pillaged citizenry—only the maturing, quiet, inner mind of a killer. His mind was used to supervise, to prepare so he could rule sitting on the throne—to replace the Pope. The money in this recent contract had to be near three million dollars. He wished he had left the Federal Bureau of Investigation after ten instead of fifteen years of a suppressed existence.

Owen's position as associate professor of history was easily provided to him because the federal government supplied grants, research money, and contracts for federal projects, and he had distributed these funds to universities. After leaving the FBI, a cover career easily started.

The Cardinal's tweed jacket, his vest, or sweater, and aromatic pipe tobacco never impressed Owen. It was his editorial and scholarly qualities that both he and the Michigan Pope admired.

The aging Pope, yes, that's the name we operatives called the head of our business, prepared to retire. He was complex. A formal, blue, dress suit or a flannel shirt with corduroy pants comfortably fit him. The Pope's mind wondered to Saudi Arabia and Uzbekistan in nanoseconds. If attention returned, no one knew, but the Pope knew and the Cardinal agreed that Owen had to make this trip, had to supply and support Poole on this hit.

All three men conspired and were complicit in this contract for murder. Only the Pope knew the contact who Owen thought to be an international lawyer. Owen tried to prove this.

Only the Pope and the Cardinal controlled the incoming money and its allocation.

Owen's offshore money accounts grew, yet subordination, sublimation, a low profile—almost a vow of poverty—lead to his acceptance that only in his old age would he spend money and then only sparingly. He had cut back on insurance premiums.

Why did he do it? This complex story is as complex as how and why this Pope controls life from Ann Arbor, Michigan. Owen and the Pope harbor deep awareness of why they kill, what brought them to this point, who benefited and who didn't, and they had no remorse. Their nature was inborn.

Owen's inability to out-think the Pope and Cardinal arose because of a lack of knowledge. One who controls knowledge wields power.

Owen contacted, controlled, commissioned the eight operatives who were from government positions—two from the Mossad, two older assassins from the Central Intelligence Agency, an Iranian, a KGB Russian, and two former FBI agents, who were Poole and Owen himself. If and when Owen moved up, the triumvirate would finalize the ongoing search for another assassin who had administrative skills as well as operative expertise. Poole could not move up. She was expert in what she did.

Her resentment made her better. Certainly her lack of knowledge further frustrated her and if it were not for Owen, the business would be less one international killer for hire. Owen would miss her. Confronted with her broad shoulders, her closeness, men were forced to want to possess her—to wrestle her to the ground, to love her. Of course, no one could. Her cat like motions held the observer's eye and her beautiful hazel eyes and blonde hair radiated like amethysts in the sand. Owen used discipline to remove her from his mind, which had started discursive sexual fabrications when she was a rookie. He was ten years older and having his third child at the time. She is forty-two now and in the prime of woman's liberative mind, spirit, body and soul.

As she does, he still weight lifts, practices Jujitsu and Karate, and runs and jumps rope. These exercises have to come to an end for him. So much surreptitious work took extra time. So much deceptive procurement; so much retentive thinking would force exercise to take a back seat—at least soon after this Spanish mission.

Smoke might rise from the chamber of the Cardinal among the buildings and trees of Ann Arbor indicating a new Pope had been picked. Owen planned to be the new Pope. Let this hit be a success. He prepared for his history lecture. Michigan had a marvelous library, and a crowded, competitive campus. This is reality.

Poole, also known as "00" in the FBI, now lived outside Dublin, Ireland. "Oo" was really "owe owe" because if Owen, who was called "O," shot a hundred percent in a weapons match at the FBI, Poole scored right after him with a ninety-nine. "Owe owe," the agents said again when they looked up at the oak bordered, cork, bulletin board. She quest unforgivingly, relentlessly to be the best in qualifications.

Now she was first, no longer in the FBI. Owen did not operate. She was in her prime; formally retired at forty-one and working for the Pope.

Owen commissioned her. She would cheat to beat anyone she considered a bastard. She broods. She harbors secrets so black that thunderstorms rumbled in her pelvis.

The transformation from agent to lady to executioner seemed natural after so many years of professional bullshit, pure struggle against men and bureaucracy, official sublimation, dislocation, paper reports, freedom of information—she wanted to black out everything—frustration, family responsibilities, a despised husband and ... these thoughts surfaced now and then and anviled down because she had found simplicity after the "calm"—which simply was now a job no one told her how to do. She aspired; she controlled. She knew none of this history would affect her Ladyship or Archery Club. The Nná would win too.

———

Late July 1998, Owen, taking on a false identity, bused to New York City and flew to Nice, France. He rode a public bus to Eze—a small hill town near the curvy route along the sea to Monaco. He walked to a glass works building, talked to a gaffer, and picked up two bulk headed packets about the size of a pack of long cigarettes. Inside one, neatly mangered and swathed in white silk, were rows of double ended *petite* glass ampules. The other, larger and insulated, was cooled below 56° fahrenheit.

The return bus stopped at the central bus depot in Nice, where he stepped into the bus to the airport. There he boarded another public bus that traveled to and through the famous towns of the French Riviera including Cannes. Ultimately, he stopped at the industrial port of Marseille where he saw to the shipment of crates and a new private sailing yacht carrying Poole's cargo. He flew from Marseille to Barcelona, Spain. He used a different passport.

Owen

From the plane looking right, loomed the tall Pyrenees Mountains. My mind envisioned a large black and white photograph of a Republican woman and child walking in cold, mountain snow. Frigid winds blew the hat and black cape of the French border soldier who carried their luggage up front.

In the Spanish Civil War 1936-39, two hundred and twenty thousand Republican supporters fled by this route from the Nationalist Army under General Franco's command. He had seized Barcelona, imprisoned and killed sympathizers. Why this picture?

It is the antithesis of my purpose. Poole's demands were procured with great difficulty within a month. Only one of the two cigarette packages was mine. The process was devotion, a homily. Maybe I wanted to escape being a procurer. Maybe in this picture I saw the worship of women—their power, their need to be protected and sheltered. Maybe I saw the continuance of life all so antithetical to my trip. Women don't understand men—at least I questioned Poole. If a man works hard to comprehend and express what an intelligent woman does, and he succeeds and follows with praise, he is still considered a worker not having any dignity.

The windswept cape of the soldier in his distinctive French uniform crossed my mind. He was burdened by her bags and very cold, yet ever protective and helpful. This distinctive border soldier and I would be put down by Poole. Accolades only come to reinforce a helpful, practical behavior. I question this attitude. Look, the soldier helped and I helped. I coordinated this contract. This requires genius in itself. Women have great expectations of men. The heavy woman making passage in the snow with the child lingered in my mind. Mothers bring their boys up to meet the expectations of women—to have them marriageable. Boys are bossed around when young—probably abused. Are we slaves? Worker bees? Yes, say old timers from behind a glass of wine and these philosophers imply the situation follows because of the procreative period of bearing and woman's time of patient, protective, politicking, proliferate control of human life. "Crazy," they say, "simply crazy."

The plane pumped up and down on a Pyrenees pocket of air. This feminine power eventually becomes signing checks, being waited upon by lawyers, chief executive officers, venture capitalists, and all as if I had nothing to do in the origin and development of my five girls. These thoughts say life is a put-down and that I have and will be put-down. Poole will do it.

Owen in Spain

Barcelona from the Mediterranean Sea of the Costa Durado has two headwater ports of which Port Olympico is east. This is the most modern with stores, marine services, and restaurants serving international cuisine near wide expanses of concrete. Within the other headwater is Port Vell Marina. It adjoins Barceloneta, an apartment area good for dining.

I ate *paella* for two with a cold beer on a hundred and twenty-five foot barge cornered and attractive with white canvas railings, white tubular stanchions and white umbrellas. It bordered the Historical Museum of Catalunya. Walking here I noticed that the old waterfront houses, stands, and buildings between the fish sculpture at Port Olympico and Barceloneta had been knocked down, removed, and replaced by a modern waterfront beach.

I felt the death rained upon the city by the Italian Air Force during the Spanish Civil War. The blackened rock from years of fleet and tanker refueling and red sand led back up to an expanse of gray slate brought to semi-life by the reflected setting sun. The continuous quarried squares ended against the backs of buildings not destroyed for the face-lifting that was necessary for the 1992 Olympics. Backs of buildings trying to be fronts and wilted black palm trees planted on the beach only added to the deathly scene.

Grooming, feeding, pruning could not restore life. Only the pulchritude of showering, semi-nude, females held my interest because life is about the perpetuation of people. The rice *paella*, hot and succulent, satisfied me, but I felt lonely.

West, next to Port Vell Marina, is Port Pau. Here several Dàrsena, wharves, with ferries, trawlers, loading and unloading cargo ships and cruise ships hinge on the monument of Columbus.

Colón returned here to Ferdinand and Isabella in 1493 with American Indians. The Monument a Colón is the southerly end of *Las Ramblas*, which is a street of wavy cement tiles, bordered by dark glazed bricks, tall green trees, and one way up and down side streets next to sidewalk-fronting old buildings. From the air, *Las Ramblas* is a swath of green Hispania trees penetrating old

167

city quarters. They lead up to the Plaza Catalunya and the modern northeast and west Barcelona.

Ramblas is a dried up and converted river filled with currents of people going down to the waterfront and then returning. Hitting and blocking other people was unavoidable. Turning to look at the miming entertainers, clowns, musicians, caricaturists, and colorful artwork was festive to the eye. News stands, ¡Hola! market-booths, flower and bird and rabbit and seashell stands— filled the sunny path. People buying, some so tired they had to sit on seats for a fee, or eat, served from restaurants, which abounded along this fascinating, peaceful, young, vibrant river of life, added to the activity. The river of people was young because of the abundance of students, youthful tourists, and playful teenagers who absorbed sun that strained to filter through quivering, rustling leaves falling individually upon the promenade.

I say young but some people say deathly because bullet holes with surrounding irregular chips of missing stone are seen on walls of old buildings. In 1936 the Nationalists tried to have soldiers from the local garrison take over Barcelona. Sniper and submachine gun fire splattered old buildings. Children and adults heard the "rut-ta-tut," "rut-ta-tut" coming from the thick branches of Hispania trees and from roofs of dirty buildings or squares and cathedrals, or alleys that bank the human river of *Ramblas*.

Yes, some say deathly because of the forced exodus of Jews and Moors and the intolerance and inquisition of the Catholic Church in conspiracy with Franco and in 1492 with Ferdinand and Isabella.

Youths don't know or find little meaning in or forget the dark events of the past. There should not be need for war. Young people feel this and see the ignorance of warmongers. *Las Ramblas* is a young vibrant river of life.

Darkness was falling and I chose not to enter the horde of *Las Ramblas* where necessary alertness prevented bumping into spellbound children or a strong T-shirted youth or an in love couple, or spread out wares and chairs.

I needed to think. History read in Ann Arbor allowed me to appreciate the industrious Catalans, their distinct language, their undying wish to be independent from Castile, their fine exported wine snubbed by fine fresh cork, their hazelnuts, their struggle to correct the backwardness that dictator Franco brought to their territory.

I gave credit to Franco for not allowing German troops to cross Spain into northern Africa during World War II. Also Jews throughout Europe and Mediterranean countries who had Spanish passports were given consideration at times by the Germans ... but enough ... I had to focus. My work during the past month of July, my coming up meeting with Poole at twenty-two hundred hours and why I walked streets in a NATO nation in Catalonia, once part of Rome and France and what I would do and what I had to do must take priority over my impression of historical oppression.

Owen

Time was near 10 p.m. I chose Avinguda de les Drassanes, which angled northwest from the Monument of Colón. I planned to use side streets. I walked parallel to *Las Ramblas* by turning right at the end of the long street. I wanted to walk as parallel to *Las Ramblas* as possible. Half the distance up the length of *Ramblas*, which is more than half a mile long, I had to make a right and left turn. The street corner had activity different from the quieter apartments I passed where people educated themselves by television.

My Palmcorder hung in a carry bag on my chest by a strap around my collar and jacket. I had dressed professionally as if still in the FBI, looking forward to Poole at the Rivoli Ramblas, which is a hotel that people easily walked into from the northeast side of the action packed walkway, especially on weekends. I had dressed in a chartered motor yacht available to me in *Port Olympico*.

I walked steadily. On my left, the street corner had a narrow bodega next to a dark bar with men lifting lighted cigarettes in their gesticulating arms. I crossed the intersection and on my right a seedy living quarters—a hotel—blocked the light and noise of

Las Ramblas. Next, a long dark archway enclosed couples talking business. Green doors opened and young women left in makeup and tight short skirts for the main action of *Ramblas*. Only yellow light, coming from the deep section of another narrow store, flooded a small section of the black street. I saw gutter water and trash by the lit curb. I walked farther up into the darker street where upon, startlingly, I was hit on the chest—pushed from the front by a young man with a skin-head haircut, black shirt, plaid pants, ankle clips, and combat boots. I felt the side ribs of a person on all fours against the back of my legs. As I fell backward—more into that yellow store light—my two arms pumped back to break the fall. I was relieved very expertly of my precious camcorder by a rear man.

I fell backward with my feet up and forward, whereupon I sat on a teenager who I would not let get away from under me. I slung my right elbow across and back into his face breaking his nose. My weight and blows immobilized him.

I snap-extended my leg to round kick the toe of my leather shoe into the extended inner knee of the front man. This ax-like force tripped him as I rolled to my right. I simultaneously pulled a cigarette weapon from the lapel pocket of my jacket.

The older man behind me looked like a bold veteran who should have stopped this kind of work years ago. He held the shoulder strap of my Palmcorder and hesitated to help his two comrades. His lack of motion allowed me to blow a glass dart solidly between his twilight eyes, hard into the bone of his forehead. The ampule, a double-ended glass dart, had mercury in the middle that gave the yellow glass the silver weight of a BB and the density for a fluid wave that would break a fine membrane upon contact. The shock released a neurotoxin through the tunnel tip into his bone and body subcutaneously. I had developed the projectile in the shape of the Concorde jet plane. If he suddenly put his hand up, the pointed rear tunnel would stick his hand or fingers and more neurotoxin would be released out the rear membrane by the rebounding tsunami of mercury. He would get a double dose. He did this. He yelled twice. He was on his knees and incapacitated in a couple of heartbeats.

I had released foot contact with the front man, so upon rolling back more fully onto the Spanish boy, who was learning his thievery trade, I looked and put my feet up. I rotated on my lower back slamming the kid below me once again with a fast karate chop while kicking to keep the strong front man from jumping or striking or getting a lock hold on me. I spread my feet and blew another cigarette. The double-ended ampule missed bone, but pierced his cheek, hitting the side of his molar teeth releasing the paralyzing neurotoxin. Glass and mercury escaped into the mucosa and tongue of his mouth.

I was relieved. This inconvenience was over. I grabbed the kid's hair and slammed his temple into the cobblestone street. He didn't move again.

My suit was wrinkled and dirty. I smelled shit. I rested sitting on the kid's body. I felt his lungs moving. People came up from the corner bar. I saw eyes and figures in the darkness.

From my inside jacket pocket I pulled out a filled, but plunger-locked, plastic syringe. The older rear man wore a white, cotton T-shirt. I ripped it down the middle and plunged the large dose of antitoxin at an angle into and below the skin of his upper chest. I thought that it's the blood serum of snake that has the antineurotoxin or the snake would be dead itself. After biting its prey, it's going to get venom toxins into its own body. It swallows its prey and the incapacitating toxin.

The black-shirted skin-head, last to get blown away, received a *new* needle deep into his back muscles after I pulled his shirt up over the back of his punk head. If the back man had AIDS, the front one wouldn't get it. I left a filled syringe of anti-toxin and information and instructions on his body.

I picked up my digital Palmcorder with its precious color LCD monitor and quickly walked up the dark street out onto crowded *Ramblas*. More people had come up from the bar and hotel to the strewn bodies.

I clutched the bag. No one had a chance of getting these miniature cassettes. They were for Poole's eyes only.

Poole

My khaki colored, tight shorts pressed and bent into my vagina. I hoped he would not notice the thin layer of flab constricted by the hem on my developed thighs. I'll stand up when he comes and rearrange myself. Another vodka on the rocks, and desire to stand will be lost. My destiny in Barcelona at this hotel, with its peaceful brown and blue ambiance, is alcohol oblivion. It is a peaceful thought. There is too much glare from background lights. Indirect lighting on liquor bottles is pretty, but too much for a small bar. I'll move. I do not want to talk to that enclosing man. Owen, where are you? My leg shook impatiently. You have never let me down. You know I can run circles around you. Don't mess with me—you simpleton ... you …

"Owen!" I put my head down. Don't show relief or happiness to have company in a foreign country.

"Poole!"

That's me. I'm not going to talk. Let him talk. Something's not right. "You smell like shit!" I talked.

"Trish, I didn't want you to wait."

"You look a mess." I looked up and down. He was close to me.

"Trish, I had trouble getting here."

"You're alive. That's all that counts." I raised my head, ready.

"Come, sit in the lounge. It will be more comfortable for you. How are you, Trish?"

I didn't want to say. A late clandestine rendezvous was the most fucking, ridiculous, asinine thing ... I don't even have a room yet.

"I have been waiting for my room since eight o'clock."

"I'll go talk to the receptionist."

"They're cleaning my room now."

"I'm sorry. The travel agent told me this was the best in the area of *Ramblas*. It's supposed to have a pool."

"Forget it, Owen. There's no pool here. Have you gotten everything I need?"

I didn't tell him.... I lied even to myself ... that ... that fuck of a second husband banged me up and left me to deal with it myself ... and I'm still recuperating. It hadn't been easy after three loved children, to deal with the abortion. That monster. What a mistake. Money and power are going to be scrambled, and I would do it.

"Trish, are you up to this? How was your trip?"

He is talking and bending closer. "Relaxing. Thank the ETA. I left Portsmith, England and arrived by ferry in Bilbao.

They picked me up in an air conditioned Mercedes and delivered me to this wood bar—the Rivoli Ramblas Hotel."

"You look wonderful after such a long drive."

I knew he was lying because my eyes were baggy, my legs were starting cellulite, and I was not fully recovered from the abortion. I tried. The woman supported me in every way and I was shooting better archery. I can't let them down. But that asshole …"

"You need a rest."

Finally, he was right. He didn't know what happened. Owen always appeared simple. I put my head down again. I talk too much, think too much, and I feel too much.

"Poole, I have done everything you asked this past month. I assembled an excellent team. Puerto Petro, that's your present destination. It is an hour ride east from the Palma airport by bus. From there you'll sail down to Palma, Mallorca, the Balearic capital. Don't dress outstandingly."

He knows nothing about woman's clothing. "Do you have my flower pot? Is it safe?"

"Of course. And here. Take this camcorder. Do your homework. I've spent four days surreptitiously photographing Mallorca, Palma, the Nortica Club, the harbor, Port Nous, and the bay. There is a large security force! Felipe is sailing this week. Next week, his father sails. Let's be strong. Let's get the job done."

Sometimes *he* talked too much. I wish he would just hold me and shut up. I remembered when we had our FBI "rah-rah" sessions before we hit an American diverse group and how we all backed each other up. Owen didn't have it now. He's too low gear, or is it me? Do I make him act differently? What does he think of me? He's talking.

"I have a meeting with the Devil at midnight on *Ramblas*."

"You're leaving? Who?"

"Yes. The Devil. The Devil and his followers."

"You Fuck!"

"That's uncalled for. God, you're spunky. Get some rest. I'll talk to the clerk."

"Where are you staying?"

"The Ambassador."

He left me. The automatic glass exit doors opened and closed sideways against yellow marble walls. He always left me just when I wanted to communicate. Bullshit. I communicate well. He smelled like he fell in shit. Why is my leg still shaking?

Owen

I walked into the current of people doing a midnight "*paseo*"—a walk. A multi torch, black, iron fixture lit the promenade. Suddenly, I had to stop at a large circle of people listening to "The Sounds of Silence." The air whistle instrument and guitars produced music like pine soap that bubbled me up, let me slide to transcend Poole's freckles, her blonde hair, her trip, and my assault. I felt she had lead in the head—fatigue.

Below the dark bordering balconies of square nineteenth century buildings, I planned to meet the Devil. I had needs and expectations. A *"duende,"* a mysterious kind of charm, pervaded among the shadows of the trees, along the tiles and curbs into the black sky only to be reflected from lit sparkling particulate matter that I call night dust.

A <u>flamenco dancer</u> grabbed my arm. White polka dots on a green dress and dangling ribbons danced in front of me. Castanets clicked. She had gregarious eyes and deep red lips, and after pushing back a bang of black hair, she asked me face-to-face if she was worth five hundred pesetas.

As she separated her light green shawl her breasts lifted and I said, "Many guineas" to present a British misconception. I had to move on.

"Such a waste from such a big country," she said. Her black eyes studied me. For reasons unknown to me, she knew I was the American.

A <u>baby faced man</u> in shorts, green top, and white visor cap hit sixteen water bottles and jars set before him like candles in a church and produced music that held a semi-circle of people at attention. I weaved behind the electrical equipment that accompanied his bottle sounds. I looked among the nightwalkers for the Devil—actually Miguel—who would be miming for money, supposedly out of work.

To my right, a <u>man in a red sombrero</u>, kneeling on an area rug, tried to play guitar and whistles simultaneously. He produced a cacophony of sour notes that never once impressed the deadpan dog in front of him. The miniature dog, also with a sombrero and red glasses on his black nose, should have lost both by rejecting the noise of the wood guitar and whistle puffs. It was a gag. Still people put pesetas in a red, flowerpot in front of the dog. This was pathetic but thematic entertainment. People pay for the deplorable.

Ramblaflor, La Vanguardia, José Maya, Centre De Diversio Familiar, public telephones, diseased trees, posted street lamps, and red *Grec* 98 flags guided my search for the Devil.

Paintings, selling for one hundred dollars at mini street galleries, displayed a bullfight, Don Quixote, clowns, fish, and balcony flower scenes. They blocked out the sex-shops, peep show *CineX*, discotheques and bars that emphasized the facings of old buildings—some covered in plastic green mesh undergoing renovations. The mesh prevented construction debris from striking walkers.

Colón, on the side of the Meridian Hotel, statued on a gray cloth-covered pedestal. His gray and dusty pantaloon snickers, socks, gray embroidered shirt, gray sailors hat and out-stretched arm, fascinated me because of spray painted detail. A beautiful woman—hair up, a Gucci bag hanging from her shoulder, slit up her Zebra dress showing gamine galore—stood under his extended arm for a photo taken by her elegantly suited escort. Colón's Genoese nose smelled cologne.

I passed a temporary tattoo set-up and walked on a Joan (Juan) Miró Art Display of black and white, red and blue tile, laid among the wavy walk blocks of *Ramblas*. To my right was the *Mercat - La Booteria* fenced in at this late hour. Young women stood by the fence. It was time to eat out—not go marketing.

Any walk farther south and I'd be approaching the flea market stalls and ultimately the statue of Columbus with its miniature elevator. I turned back after passing the International Hotel with its small rooms and entered into the horde of people wearing sneakers or sandals, shorts, and simple shirts. I stopped at the Bride.

She swished a large white gown that had a noticeable, shiny, satin hem at shoe level.

Of course, the white shoes could only be seen when she lifted the sprawling material toward the long green stem of a white orchid she held across her tan chest. From between large red lips, of a white-caked face, she invited children to stand with her for pictures.

Woman and children circulated around her, entranced by her smile, augmenting the wonders and sanctity and gayety of marriage.

Defaced and ripped posters that advertised soccer, music, and theater on lampposts defiled the beauty of the Bride.

Up the walk, there was less lighting because black-building walls, instead of lit shops, presented their sides to *Ramblas*. An Indian covered completely in brown make-up stood barefoot on a brown blanket. Brown leggings, a lacquered white gull-feathered head-dress over long brown hair were complimented by holding a brown spear. People gathered and the petrified miming Indian abruptly stamped the handle of the spear resonantly into the street tiles. This startled the children and they ran. Then, after another dead poise, he lifted the spear into a throwing position. Even I wanted to get away!

Turning up the wide walk I passed Darth Vader. He stood statuesque in a black robe, making the statement that he protected and defended the powerful people. Next, a Visigoth, although he could have been a pilgrim going to Santiago de Compostela five hundred miles west in Galacia or a drifter because his left hand held a long walking stick, which at the top end had a water skin and belongings. He could have been a Moore. His right hand rested on a scabbard. His maroon sash and gold pantaloon and skullcap and black mustache looked Visigoth. Besides, the Visigoths established their court in Barcelona in 415 A.D. Of course a mime doesn't talk so I felt like one of my students. I threw a two hundred-peseta coin below his gold ballerina type shoes hoping he would answer my question. As you know, he didn't, or I wouldn't be confused.

You'll think I have stopped looking for the Devil, but there seemed a unification to existence on *Ramblas*, more than met the eye.

A <u>Spanish Lady</u> of wealth—she wore her white pearls beneath a white parasol—arranged her white-fringed dress on a milk box. She looked like the ugly dominating Queen Maria Luisa of the late seventeen hundreds, only she was shorter.

A <u>clown</u>—a strong man with a cherry nose and a red curly wig, tickled the bare backs of woman with a feather, and when one turned he honked a horn and smiled and talked and entertained her.

A black top hat on an intellectual's head, adorned with spectacles, stuck up out of the backrest of a red cushioned chair. The "<u>Head</u>" had a miniature, false torso and legs with disproportionately large black shoes resting on the seat pillow. His real body sat in a covered box under the small red cushioned armchair. Interesting. Toulouse Leutrec, did he come here?

It was after midnight. Where was he? The Devil. I passed a man in ghostly, white garb; even his guitar and cello were white. <u>Pablo Casals,</u> I thought.

A modern artist, impersonating <u>Picasso,</u> painted people in cubes, squares, parallelograms, any geometric pattern, some moving in and out of hard, brightly colored, mesmerizing corners on canvas. Was I in the real world? What life other than *Ramblas* do these entertainers have? Motorcycles and bikes stood close by.

The tall Spanish trees went up a few stories, hovered over *Ramblas* in the black sky and hid the illuminated passage and the unheard Metro, deep below.

Torchlights, grouped or single, shadowed all this activity. Theaters, palaces, the library, the opera house, and museums were close to the promenade. Cathedrals and squares—squatting among tenements—filled with walking tourists. Catalans, Spaniards from Valencia, Seville, and Andalusia—from everywhere—roamed the streets. At night all seemed peaceful, but I knew better.

I approached the <u>Devil</u>. He sat covered in black cloth drapery, gray gloves with holes at the fingertips, a black towel hood, and a red hard plastic mask with two miniature horns. Large white lower front teeth over ran the upper lip. Opposite, high up, facing him, stood a female dummy, not a mime as I could detect. She had a blue dress, white scarf-shawl, long white wings, and held a black sledgehammer in white gloves, and wore a blonde wig. An archangel I assumed. Between them sat two tin cans for money. Miguel was unemployed. Two cans for one person and filling fast, stated his ambition.

I checked out the angel's stuffed white gloves. She was a thin mannequin placed high on a covered crate. I could not see straight into the eye slits of her white mask. They looked hollow from below. I looked through the holes into the dark space of a forehead.

I circled the devil. No movement. Excellent petrification, but I looked straight through the eyeholes of his red mask and saw blood shot eyes, really gross, with spidery red capillaries. I looked up to the dummy girl to make sure she was not alive and back to the Devil's eyes, which flickered.

"Got you," I said. He didn't move his eyes again. Stubborn. He knew it was I, Owen.

I picked up the shiny tin can and put a five hundred-peseta piece in it, shook it to make coin noise—telling him I was here for our meeting. Still, he did not move.

I was ten minutes late, true, but I had not seen him when I passed down this way at midnight. What did the young man want me to do? The Devil didn't move. Not a pleat in his black cape or hood changed position. No acknowledgment, and we had worked together in anti-terrorist activity before the Olympics. Was he showing me how good he was?

Suddenly, in pantomime, he rotated while sitting on the small stool. Disjunctively he stuck his gray-gloved hand, black arm, up and out, for me to shake. So I shook it feeling his fingertips. His grip was tight. He wasn't going to let go, or show emotion, but he emphasized his strength. He shook up and down robotically. He clutched my hand. He demonstrated power. He pulled me as if he were a wound-up toy with a key in its back. I had to lean closer. My left hand grabbed his right biceps and triceps and felt rippling muscles developed longer and stronger than mine. He startlingly pulled me off balance; I fell upon him. The stool overturned.

We lay on *Ramblas,* I in his robes with my face against the marbled, red plastic of the Devil's face. He held me. My knee reflexively drove into his groin. I was in the clutches of the Devil—Miguel—leader of the underground!

I detected in my peripheral vision the blue dress move above and behind to my right. The blow sounded and felt like an unbreakable acorn being hit with a hammer on concrete.

Then concentric circles in third dimension telescoped me into the funnel of a descending thunderstorm, a bulging vortex of boiling fluid, dynamic circles in and out, colored clouds of gun smoke—Goyer's 1808 painting of the French Execution of Spaniards—spots, splotches, and I was unconscious.

"Ha. Owen. Señor. Stay still. Ha. You are working. Don't move. The *policia* will come if … No Señor. *Gracias*. Lie still."

I lay prostrate, the red mask on me now, and the black robe over me. Miguel, not stirring except for his lips, held the sledgehammer to my head. People were about, putting coins into a hat.

He wore the female dummy's yellow wig and a black turtleneck shirt. The Devil had defeated the devil, but no pedestrian understood the irony. All they saw is that someone had beaten a devil. Is not that what I was here for? I was my own Don Quixote.

"Señor. Sorry. *Por favor*. Rest. You hear me? You work now. You feel better?"

His words filtered down through the red devil's mask, beyond my clenched eyes, into the headache and out the side of my head where I had been struck with a tap from the heavy sledgehammer.

"It was <u>Mimi</u>. She say you worked me with your knee, that I was in danger. Ha. No, I told her. Owen no hurt me. We are friends. Men do this.… She go—take everything—chair, coins, motorcycle. Ha, she is the best mime on the street. Loyal. Very loyal, alert, protective, motherly, she is the Madonna of the Holy Family. Madonna *mia*. *Lo siento*, sorry.

"Stay, Owen. We are making money. <u>Diego</u> will come. He works at the Ambassador up the street. Ha. He and I will help you."

I clenched my eyes more. Only black and white, no more color. The pain lessened slightly. What a day! At least I had a hotel reservation at the Ambassador. The Dream Team slept there in nineteen ninety two-two-two …

I woke up in what seemed a quadruple double bed. A young, athletic man looked down upon me inquisitively. His large head pedestaled above his black service vest. His shirt collar was too big for his brown, lean, muscular neck.

"Sir, I am Diego." He turned his torso like a bullfighter, a Torero. "It is my pleasure to help America."

00, where are you? I'm with a bunch of dilettantes.

"No Señor. I am Diego. Cuban. I help you." He read my mind.

"Morphine," I blunted.

"No Sir, but maybe soon. A woman is here for you."

Poole. It had to be Poole. My wife only comes for the girls. Trish, Trish PooUle, oollle ...

When I awoke, I found a warm spot for my calvaria to settle supported in the pillows. I didn't dare move.

Trish wore a black full-length dress designed with a very low-cut back that opened onto the end of the hard, flat, slide of flesh that I like to feel. The elegant dress had a high slit up the side and spaghetti shoulder straps. Her chest and straightforward nipple breasts squarely confronted every person and problem in the room. Swiftly she sat next to my arm. Good. She did it gently, athletically.

"These are ibuprofen, 0. Drink. Sleep. I'll be here."

I did it. She dabbed the blood clot in my hair. I was going under for the fourth time. God, I'll never hurt another person again. Wicked. An innocent over-reaction, Mimi? I forgive you, if I live.

Poole

Diego talked boldly, adventursomely. He had brown skin handsomeness. His close haircut on the sides of his head, clean shaven face splashed with aftershave, sinewy muscles, and intelligent sparkling eyes made him a "torero" ready to direct the awesome power of a bull. I pulled the black straps off my shoulders. The dress pulled down. I wanted to get out of it. I was as tired as Owen. I needed to talk—to sleep. How does one do both simultaneously? She dreams.

"Señora, I am a baseball player, from Cuba. I practice my English with you. *Si*?"

And he posed at the foot of the bed. His knee was up high in front of his chest; his long arm with the smooth strength of a boa constrictor extended back with twisted wrist for unwinding power; his long fingers manipulated an imaginary sown leather ball in a configuration necessary for an awesome ready-to-deliver pitch. His service vest bulged on the left side. Wow! What a man. His wholesome face looked at me but his mind never saw a woman, only a strike zone.

"I'll be in New York in one more year. I must become a Spanish citizen first to enter the United States and qualify for the big-er league. You like?"

"How old are you?"

"Twenty-two. See? I play Barcelona ball." He turned his wrist, cocked it, lifted his thigh and leg high and threw an imaginary white baseball. His shoulders and back were lean and awesome.

"Good, Diego. But go get some food for us now and champagne for me." My mind knew we needed this youth somewhere, but my body belonged with Owen whose warmth, his ... I started unconsciously to disrobe. Diego got out of himself and left quietly and quickly.

I pulled my side bedspread and blanket down. The light was still on. I pulled up snug to the lug. He never saw my black dress or my perfect choke pearls. He breathed deeply. This is another kettle of fish; he snored. Heavy eyelids darkened the hotel room.

Owen, next day

"Mimi say, forgive her. She will practice this week and help. Ha. I use in escape. I pass Señora in street. She say, 'You still sleep. No good for her.' She say, 'Dogs are horses in this city.' She was cleaning her high heels by a dumpster. Knock-out, as you say, Sir."

"Miguel, close the drapes. The afternoon sun splits my head. Put a wall light on. Do you have information for me?"

"Yes, Owen, and I want to discuss many thing with you."

They heard a knock at the door.

Diego came into the bedroom and held Owen's washed and pressed suit high like a matador after the bull passes. "Señor, it smelled like Old Havana. I take out wood cigarette case from pocket and put lapel cigarettes in case. Your knife, wallet, syringe, all safe."

"*Gracias*. Miguel says that you are an important member of the team. I am grateful."

"I help you. I be in America next year. I talk English."

"Ha, Diego, go buy 'Tic-Tacs' for the American."

"*Si*. I bring food in two hours. Here, some from last night. 'Tic-Tac, Tic-Tac,'" he repeated as he left gracefully.

"He will be another El Duque for the Yankees. Fine man. Ha. Courageous."

"Miguel, who wants to kill His Majesty King Juan Carlos? Did you go to Estoril, Portugal? I want to discuss the reason behind this entire plan because my research does not indicate a need, even an unreasonable reason for his elimination. The Basques, ETA, will sign a peace accord with Madrid soon. The Catalans, though anti-Castilian, are semi autonomous and smart to descent from their nationalism. Tourism has opened the country to globalization. The European Economic Community is of great help. NATO participation makes Juan Carlos's position as Commander in Chief more important. His navy has an aircraft carrier. He and Queen Sophia encourage the arts. He presents a handsome figure for the monarchy with his broad blue, diagonal ribbon, red waist sash, and medalled uniform. He is the final protector of the constitutional government!"

Miguel, his strong vertical torso like a British Harrier jet ready for vertical take off, started pacing at the foot of the bed.

"*Si*. He is so wealthy. We are poor—unemployed. You help us; we help you. We never like the secrecy of the king. Such polarization, but we would not kill him."

"So who? What happened in Estoril?"

"In 1956, ha, he killed Alphonso, his younger brother."

"Accidentally."

"We don't know for sure. Ha. Such an accident allowed him unchallenged claim, training by Franco, to assume the right of succession."

"Are there resentful family members? His father Don Carlos de Bourbon may have had reason. He died in 1993. He had been passed over by Franco."

"No. It was he, ha, who introduced his son to yachtsmanship, democracy, and guided him."

"What about Americans, Miguel?"

"Possible. There is the Juan Carlos Hilton close by. Billions have been put into this country. Bankers and investors consult Juan Carlos. This is costly."

"Could it be Felipe, his son?"

"It is the secrecy that we don't like. We the people have no real say when it comes to big decisions such as airports, military and civil, trains ... All these investments are big money. Spanish General Motors is the fourth biggest European car producer. Ford, General Electric, Westinghouse are here. What can we read in the newspapers? One of the problems where local control is lost is that the Cortes, the legislative branch, is still able to nationally do what it wants under the call-to-assembly by the king. Ha. Felipe is next king. He is in no hurry."

"I can't find reason nor sympathy for this mission. Why is beyond me. What about unions?"

"They are never happy, yet they do work with the government. Ha. There is a great resentment from workers for the taxation necessary to present the 1992 Seville World Fair and the Barcelona Olympics. Every day they pay for these billions unhappily. Ha, but if it were not for the Guardia Civil, Army, and police, they would do it themselves."

"So it could be the workers?"

"It is hard to say. Ha. If you're working, you're fortunate in Spain. Si, also you Señor are expensive. Si?"

"Miguel, ironically, I don't like the secrecy of my own associates. I live in a small Spain myself. I want to know more."

"But, you have much money. I need twenty thousand more to continue the plan. Señora is very elaborate. She is our Evita—our Lady of Hope."

"Puff up my pillow. I don't want to move yet, but I feel slightly better. This sledgehammer blow I hope has not caused any internal hemorrhage. I have given Mimi the last name Meninges – pia, dura mater, and aracknoid – an anatomical name instead of a street name that comes to mind. What about Lanzarote, the Canary Island? Any neighbors who would want to do him in?"

"Ha. I sent the 'Head' to the island. King Juan Carlos owns a villa on Costa Teguise above Arrecife and is well received. No. He lives swanky.

"Owen, let us aim for Sunday. Ha. There will be a fleet of sailboats on the water. Church-going Catholics and tourists will provide adequate cover."

"Fine. I must rest for two or three more days. Contact the yacht at Puerto Petro, Mallorca. Make sure everything is delivered and in top working condition. I'll have 00 bring your money. Drill the team. Is the missile launcher ready? Make sure 00 can handle it in her sleep! Give me the ibuprofen. Miguel, delay the food until 00 returns. She'll call service for Diego. I must rest. It's a burning headache."

"Si Señor. *Buenos tardes*. I take Poole to empty textile warehouse after our morning meeting. *Mañana*."

Poole

"Murder is entertaining, Miguel, isn't it?"

"Si, Señora."

"You entertain on *Ramblas*. What entertains you, Miguel?"

"Being here helping you, Señora. Take the launcher tube and lay it here on your right shoulder. Ha. Look through the viewer and aim the sight hairs. If manual or optical, estimate yardage and raise the tube relative to the horizon. Note the ladder gauge. For short distances, make sure you know that the heat seeking ability is off in the missile as well as buttons here by the trigger. In Afghanistan, we had trouble. Again, Señora, widen your stance."

"You have a good grip, Miguel."

"Of course if the diesel on the boat is running hot and is isolated, leave all the heat activators on."

"I prefer a forty-five caliber pistol."

"Si, but shots either by pistol or rifle will be picked up by sensors. Distance from the sensors is measure by Doppler effect. By circular triangulation on a map, you will be found if within a mile of the security boats and land stations. A missile launcher sounds like a splash and will be less detectable."

"There are suppressers. Did I order any?"

"No, Señora."

"Can Owen shoot this thing?"

"Si, Poole, he is good."

"Let's practice more. You are a good instructor, Miguel. To find you are the Devil is intriguing. Are you available for sex?"

"Señora Poole, he will be better soon. Ha. Mimi is mine. Lift - place - aim - fire. You will be good, Señora. If you use laser sight, you must keep it on target until explosion. Spread your legs more. The missile travels along the laser beam."

"Am I stable enough, Miguel?"

195

Diego brought lunch and "tic-tacs" to Owen's room with the air of a matador. He left quietly. Owen had time to think about his relationship with Poole.

She had stayed last night again and was expected back any minute from her practice with Miguel. 0 thought 00 should sleep at the Rivoli Hotel. Some women don't understand men, he thought. They have such unreasonable expectations of men. Money calms a good percentage.

An intermittent headache remained. His test for cure was to blow "tic-tacs" through the wall light shade until he broke the bulb. He would be healthy again. Tomorrow would be the day of the test. Do Queen Sophia and King Juan Carlos make love?

Poole

It's erotic suffering. My husband spurns me, and he is not smart enough to hide it. I am rejected by a "caballero" turned terrorist. I am not even considered by birdbrain Owen. My three children are absent and 0 wants me to think about who paid the Pope for this assassination. Di is dead. It's Juan's time. It's bloody simple. I hope Charles isn't playing with the king. I hate unnecessary bloodshed, but people, if they are not smart enough to know with whom they should associate, will pay with consequences and I have planned this as a grand "tercio de muerte"—death phase.

"Ah, 0, you're sitting upright in bed. Miguel is a good worker. He called Mallorca and the French crew has been playing with my toys. Miguel is worried and will send Darth Vader and the 'Head' to Puerto Petro to quiet the escape motor and settle the French crew. They will test all navigation equipment and check provisioning, fuel, and water. They will place ammunition and weapons on the crafts. The launcher is heavy. I didn't know there were so many ways to aim a missile. I'll shower here."

"Missiles can also be aimed by radar and there are active and passive homing," said Owen. "Are you prepared, 00? Everyone seems to know his or her position and job. This morning Miguel, Diego, and some members of the team were here. The mini bar is empty. The bride is a gutsy anarchist. Instead of her, the flamenco woman will meet you at the Palma fuel pumps.

"There is a member, a <u>Moor</u>, who'll be crew on the king's racing yacht. He will visually track your position and try to expedite the safety of the crew. He admitted that forward on the bow he couldn't do much but set an example of how to get out of your way."

"He better be a cock of the walk," said Poole.

"He controls half the crew. The sail setters, changers, the storage crew, grinders will listen—all forward people sitting ballast on the toe rail. He thinks only the navigator or tactician, and king will be destroyed. He will try. It's the only part of your plan I have trouble with along with your escape. Can you fire that missile launcher accurately?"

"Owen, it's going down. I'm taking the ferry to Mallorca tomorrow and a bus to Puerto Petro to work on camouflage. Have Miguel bring the UHF handheld talkabouts. If you drive along the coast, you'll be able to contact me. No, instead have the red-nosed clown do this. I like to be tickled as I move. Radio range is five miles, so make him think of the maximum distance I can travel and stay within it. I am going to Amaya Restaurant tonight. Shall I bring food back for you?"

"No, Diego is showing me how to fall forward off the mound. He is a striking waiter."

"He's handsome and Miguel is a gentleman. But fuck, Owen, all of you better work out my plan."

"Trish, they're going to Palma, Mallorca on Saturday by speed boat. The 'Head' and Darth Vader will help you earlier; afterward they will set up positions east of Palma. Dali, Picasso, Casals and Sombrero are there now planning tactics, escape routes, diversionary affairs, even dinner for all of us Saturday night on the fourth floor of the Joan of Arc restaurant in Palma."

"You are right, 0. They are committed. When was your last bath? Remember Magen's Bay, St. Thomas on anti drug trafficking? We spent a lot of nude time together on ATT property. Those guys wouldn't leave us alone."

"They were a pain in the ass. We should have been investigating anti-communications. That would have kept them inside. It was fun, Trish."

"Come in. The steam warmed up the bathroom. I'll hold your head."

"Do a dance. Let me see those stems."

"Only if you'll get out of bed."

"Trish, if I have any clots, I want them to stick to my skull. An embolism or stroke I don't need."

"You owe me, Owen, I thought a future with you would be fun as well as work. Actually, you need a CAT scan."

"Maybe tomorrow morning, before you're off, I'll give you all the support I can muster," said Owen.

"I am holding you to that. It's been a frustrating year."

Poole

I got on Transmediterránea Ferry. A low level mistral blew and I expected waves.

High-pressure air was expected and it would calm the seas by Sunday. My smile kept men away instead of holding their interest. Owen had satisfied me sexually. Through me, other men knew Owen was the man.

Owen

I paid for the shade, bulb, and pitted wall. My cheeks and neck had expanded and pressure did not affect my head. My checkout on Thursday was the day after Poole's, but she was still with me on flight lB1718 Iberia *destin* Palma De Mallorca. Her fluids bathed me even now. I felt them in my mind lubricating, caressing, and bringing me up to life's greatest pleasure. She had not left me and wouldn't. I've done everything I could to satisfy her. What's left?

Owen

"Father, last week on my visit to *Sa Seu*, Palma Cathedral, I told you I would return with my donation."

The priest climbed to the top of a tall stepladder held by an acolyte and turned on an off light. This was one of the lamps that adorned the altar below architect Gaudi's wrought-iron canopy. The canopy looked like a purse fishing net flung forward high into the broad nave, held in suspension to capture the Holy Ghost and to keep him here to be played upon by dazzling, colored light from circular rose windows.

"In a moment, my son. To clean beyond the reach of a woman is a man's devotion."

I thought, to clean this gothic, elegant church of such a magnificent scale would take an army. The cathedral filled with people for the next mass. The choir stalls started to fill with singers in white and red cassocks.

"Ascend to the museum. I'll be with you shortly," he bellowed down.

I felt impatient. It was ten o'clock Sunday morning and the underground team had emerged. Any minute Poole would be sailing into the harbor for fuel. I wanted to see through my telescope what "His Majesty The King's International Cup" looked like. What did Juan Carlos I resemble at the helm?

"Father, I'll hold the ladder for you."

Poole

Puerto Petro is quiet and beautiful at sunrise. A navigator can establish the error of her marine compass by taking a line on the sun over her compass. That is either now, or in the evening, when the sun's lower limb is one-half the diameter of the sun above the horizon. At this visual height, the sun is actually at sunrise or sunset. Refraction causes a low sun to appear higher. Compare the compass line bearing with the sun's true bearing found in the yearly nautical almanac for that time and latitude. The difference in degrees is the mistake of the compass induced upon it by earth's magnetic fields as well as onboard magnetic effects for the compass direction of your boat. My first husband, who sailed

Lake Michigan, taught me this concept of Amplitude and I will never hold it against him. My compass has to be perfect.

Owen, I am staring at a pink, two-story building with green, closed, louvered shutters. A yellow mailbox, a new black motorcycle, and a symmetrical green tree blocked sections of the front wall. The view reminds me of you. You're solid, brilliant, and beautiful. It hurts to say that you coordinated perfectly. We painted anything black that was light or reflective on the escape boat, and added blue and green. We suppressed the engine noise. Darth Vader and the 'Head' are no longer here. The French crew left. Only Colón and I remain ready to leave. He still poses, keeping his arms up and out in enlightened discovery, pointing to the New World. His trousers and stockings, sailor's cap, and big face are spray-painted gray. He is silent.

Colón steered the Beneteau Clipper, sparkling and white, east—past the watchtower into the Mediterranean Sea. The quiet diesel engine maintained the calm of the town.

"True course 224°," I said, while putting on sun block in chap lip balm.

"Deviation, Señora?"

"3° West."

"Compass Course 228°, Señora."

He knew basic piloting. Variation is 1° 12' West. I wanted to see his seamanship. "The mainsail, Colón," I ordered.

"Si." He faced the bow off the southeast wind, used the wheel lock on the binnacle, stepped forward, released the rope clutch on the cabin deck, and pulled out the furled-in-mast mainsail. The wind filled the mainsail making pull easier.

Years ago I had to face into the wind to raise the mainsail. Colón's strong shoulders, completed the hoist by wrenching the main halyard line without leaving the cockpit. He wrenched the outhaul line attached to the clew of the mainsail. Within seconds he locked the clutch, neatly coiled the lines, and stood miming on course at the helm.

"Speed, Colón?"

"6.5 knots."

I brought my notes from the chart desk. "Keep speed and compass course 228° for one hour and twenty-eight minutes. Change to compass course 305° between Cabera Island and Cape Salines and travel three more hours. Change to compass course 348° with Cape Regana abeam. Estimated time of arrival Port of Palma is eleven hundred hours. Here is a coastal chart with a dead reckoning track."

He pressed a button after screwing his Rolex. Rolex chronograph? I had missed the wristwatch under the ruffle of his shirtsleeve. The 'Head' said Colón sailed Sardinia.

Hum, and I give instructions! There are the Swan World Championship, Swan Rolex regattas, and the biennial Sardinia Cup held on the emerald Costa Smeralda. My expectations increased. He has probably sailed these races.

"Colón, tonight my escape will be hell. I'm going below to sleep."

His broad gray nose faced the apparent wind almost straight on. He motor sailed handsomely, petrified and salty gray behind the stainless steel wheel. Aft, behind him, our wrapped cargo lay suspended and lashed to the reversed transom.

Hours later I came up the companionway into the cockpit. The French crew had removed the cockpit table, leaving an empty square area in front of the binnacle. Immediately, the tied cargo reminded me of the work to come. But our wake was larger, out of order for this boat, so I looked at Colón. He had a large smile on his face. His left hand was moving left and right on the wheel. His right hand pulled and pinched at the guy line to his right, which turned ninety degrees from a transom corner block and a starboard winch. My eyes followed the guy line forward. I saw the cliffs and beaches of Mallorca behind the guy, but my eyes lit up to the front of the clipper.

Above me, on the left, the white mainsail and genoa vibrated. At the end of the guy were a shackle, a pole, and a large blue and red triangular sail—the chute. Its high sky position pulled us downwind with the power of a mule. All the wind pushed us. Everything was silent. The sun emblazoned the three sails, the wind bellowed, and Colón glided in heaven. Our entry into the Bay of Palma felt magnificent.

"There is Palma, Mallorca!"

"Si, Señora. The cathedral rises to the sky, man's adoration of God. The sun glorifies His presence. Do you hear the bells?"

"Yes. Yes, I do."

"The Belfries. Here, Señora, handle the afterguy."

I took the line and kept the chute—which is like a spinnaker—full, deep, up, and out. I didn't want to spill the wind and have it collapse. I had to concentrate on the outer luff edge of the sail so if it curled from lighter air, I had to jerk it. I constantly played with the sail tack corner, by way of the guy, checked the mast head wind indicator, and observed ripples on the water. Colon had been doing this as an aside. The boat kept shifting its course making control difficult. Puffs of wind startled me.

"What's our course, Colón?"

"348°, Señora. I beg your pardon; we are an hour early. I am going forward to douse the parachute."

I took over the helm. Balancing the guy and the wheel and feeling the responsibility of a captain momentarily caused me to mime! I must keep a downwind course.

The gray seaman went along the starboard railing, lowered the pivoting end of the pole on the front of the mast, and walked the pole length forward to the head stay. The chute now to port

205

was blanketed from the wind by the genoa and the winged-out main.

Colon released the guy snap shackle so the chute's luff flew out free. I had one less job. Or did I?

I moved left from behind the wheel and relieved the winched sheet that came from the clew opposite the tack on the foot of the chute. This line had a knot in it so as it ran forward, if it ever released from the winch near me, the knot acted as a stop at its lead block and the chute wouldn't go off like an octopus in the air. Colón pulled down and forward as he smothered the attached light nylon sail on the deck. At the same time he lowered the chute's masthead halyard at the rate he doused the chute. I'll miss the mule, this red and blue sail that made our entry into and through Palma Bay an impressive presentation.

I continued downwind in the bay toward the harbor. My ex-husband and Owen would be proud of me. While Colon bagged the chute, I looked up to the light brown nineteenth century tower of the cathedral. Owen would be looking through the round windows and coordinating by a UHF hand held receiver-transmitter.

Why was I doing this and the future act? I wanted to tell Owen that it was for him and for the destruction of men who think they can get away with greed and lack of sincerity; for the destruction of men who with the nonchalance of their head nod and with cold objectivity, oppress and take advantage of people;

it was to clean up the world of the immoral and badly emotionally deranged. I thought of our president.

Owen never underestimated the mind, but I don't know if he ever felt the mind. Time will come when justice, righteousness, compassion, and understanding prevail. Hell to those who don't comply.

"Señora, Señora, 348° por favor. The west harbor breakwater!"

"I have control, Colón." He was furling the genoa and mainsail from the cockpit using the many colored Dacron lines, the winches and black clutches on either side of the companionway. There were many unloading container ships on the east, *levante* dike. Exiting pleasure yachts passed our way. The quiet diesel that I turned on propelled our new white clipper into the crowded harbor by piercing the water between the massive west and east breakwaters.

I put a babushka on to control my hair. Colón, with the Clipper near the fuel pier, tried to position the yacht among charter boats. We were protected from the bay by the east breakwater. We needed traffic control.

"Circle more, Colón," I said, looking at my wristwatch.

Slowly and carefully with a pantomiming nod of his sailor cap towards the other captains, he turned, passed up a chance to move in, and let other boaters dock beam-on for gas or diesel.

207

On the dock stood only one gas and one diesel pump about one hundred feet apart. At least seven yachts circled for entry. One from the harbor direction tried and succeeded squeezing to the dock ahead of the patient circling boats. I, as a quirk, respected that. Alternatively, young men in summer clothes, yelling and having fun on a chartered powerboat gave up and went to Port Pi within the west breakwater. They came back restless, having been sent on a wild goose chase. It's a submarine weapons school.

"Do you see the Flamenco dancer?"

"Si. She stands unusually still against the back of the dock kiosk, holding a tall flower pot tightly against her dress."

"What is the temperature, Colón? I hope she has watered the plant."

"She has, Señora. Everything is rehearsed. She has balance of a ballerina, strength of a man. She will be safe. We put the Bride on Avinguda Gabriel Roca to block traffic and protect Diego. The Bride is difficult to control. Armed with an Uzi under her gown, she is volatile but capable to take on a platoon of police. She promised Miguel she would follow Owen's orders from the Belfries. Do you feel any tensions, Señora?"

"Yes. Let us approach the pier now. The sleep helped and when I go into action, I focus and nobody or anything gets in my way."

"*Muy – bueno, Señora. Si.*"

After fueling and receiving the flowerpot, we passed the clipper through the east and west harbor *diques* out into the open bay of Palma. Down in the salon I had puffed pillows around the flowerpot. The high plant package consisted of a stockade of machined cylindrical rods held together by interwoven string. Inside were two tall curved plastic limbs and one irregular joining piece. These held the foil that protected the fine long stem roses planted deeply in the soil.

I put on my camouflage wet suit, letting the goggles hang on the back of my neck. I laid Colón's flippers, facemask, wet suit, thermals, tanks, and regulator on the salon bunk so he could easily transform into a frogman.

I decided to disassemble the rose package. I put together the three tall plastic pieces, using two special lock bolts, tested the assembly and laid it flat on the forward cabin berth. I unwound the string woven throughout the stockade, attached it to the cam and idler ends of the three connected plastic pieces, tested it by strumming, and laid it on the berth. The stockade was in disarray but the roses looked gorgeous, sturdy, and ready to be picked.

I had discarded the idea of sniper fire because of the movement of the two boats and because of detection and difficulty of escape. Yet, I was excellent at one thousand yards on land with a Winchester, scope, and the right ammo. No one in the US Army could outshoot me.

The clipper hit a little chop and a moment of fear whelmed up and settled inside me. I packed the pillows around the roses.

"Lady, Señora, look, two miles forward ... left."

I stepped to the port coaming of the cockpit. Through the image-stabilizing binoculars I saw what looked like a landing armada. A fleet of modern sailing racers, between twenty-seven and eighty feet hull lengths, beat under vortices of wind to approach and round a windward marker off Cove Estanced and the beach of Palma—the north shore of the bay.

Out of place for any Sunday regatta was the tilting and swaying black helicopter, which moved up and down the line, and the two awesome black, outstanding frigates—one on the beach side headed counter to the line and the other on our side moving with the queue of sails. Taking up the rear, motor yachts and various powerboats full of onlookers, commissioners, committee members and referees kept up, interested.

"Those are fast attack craft with surface-to-surface missiles, torpedo tubes, and seventy-six and forty millimeter weapons.

"Just great." This scene was not on any cassette.

"Owen. Come in. Owen, do you hear me? Over."

"Yes, Trish. You're doing fine. Pass left of the anchored freight ship. You are parallel and behind the regatta. Do you see the sails?"

"Yes, you bastard! Two fast attack craft with missiles, one with a helicopter pad on the stern and a seventy-six millimeter gun on the foredeck. That's a frigen frigate."

"Only one black helicopter today. You can handle it. Be careful of the red coastal-patrol helicopter up the east coast."

"Owen, you owe me. There could be a submarine here for all I know!"

"Everyone's in place. Communication using the handholds is excellent from the cathedral. I just hope the bells don't go off again. My bones vibrate."

"It serves you right. Next time I am doing the reconnoitering."

"Señora, look up. It's Sombrero, Casals, and Dali. Casals is teaching Sombrero how to play the cello." The black side of the freighter hull hovered above us. "They must be entertaining the skeleton crew or the rally. Look, Señora! Dali's mustache is wrapping around the wires of the loudspeakers. His watch hangs distortedly like a giant, fried egg over the toe rail. There's Sombrero's stoic dog looking down with red glasses on his snout."

"Owen. Come in. Are you being funny? Come in."

"Stay tuned, Trish. Faith."

"The smaller boat classes are rounding the marker to their starboard. We will be at a right angle to them. We are going to cross their path in twenty minutes, Señora. Is this what you want?"

"Exactly, Colón." I started unwrapping the rear cargo. I laid the missile launcher on the floor of the cockpit. I opened a box of rear-loading missiles. I removed the canvas cover from the cargo. When I looked up I saw in one view at least sixty racing sailboats crossing our bow a quarter of a mile ahead. To the left was a stream of boats, at least two hundred, coming up to the marker, turning, and intersecting our course to Cape Enderrocat. You couldn't miss what looked like Word War II naval vessels. The racing boats were some distance off. Their sails, silver and copper fish scales, zippered across our view.

"We will be among them soon, Colón. Don't interfere. Avoid their barrage. In fact we are going to join them. We are entering the race!"

The attack craft started looking bigger. They certainly maneuvered. The king's security temporarily overwhelmed me. We were among the racers in the fleet.

"There's the king. It's the maxi. See the group of long and taller sloops to the rear of the line? He is turning to his starboard."

"Yes, Colón. Do you hear that?"

"It's music, Señora, amplified from the anchored freighter. It's cello, whistles, and guitar."

"No, that?"

"Yes. It's gunfire from the harbor, Señora. Probably the Bride is using her Uzi in the streets on the king's soldiers. Look back. See the smoke below the windmill along the bicycle path of Avinguda Gabriel Roca? Diego is throwing smoke canisters all along the semi-circle of the harbor. The Bride and he will draw the army, Guardia Civil, and police up into Avinguda Joan Miró and ultimately the grounds of the Bellever Castle. They'll escape."

"Colon! Watch that boat." Crossing our bow a crew of about eleven hiked to port, all in yellow uniform racing shirts. Colon diverted left into hundreds of oncoming sailboats. "We are in their way. Turn to starboard, Colón. Let out the mainsheet. Release more wind. Join them."

"Si. Coming about, Señora. We are ahead of the king. He'll be pulling up to our starboard quarter. Magnificent yacht compared to those in the smaller classes. Look ahead, toward the mark off Sec Island, below Cape of the Cave of Figuera. What a view of reflected light from copper and silver sails."

I turned forward from looking to the king's racing sloop, which had twenty sailors on the windward rail. A giant cloud of white smoke rose from the water up into the clear, blue sky ahead of the fleet.

"It is the Indian and the Visigoth. They have a smoke generator on a speedboat. They are motoring against and into the fleet. They'll be here and beyond in five minutes. I must get my scuba gear on." He jumped below.

At the wheel, I didn't have time to think or speak to Owen. He worked.

Already the clear sky showed brilliant fire works—yellow bursts, red bursts, pop, crackle and pop. The sky filled with the greatest showering colored display I had seen. The frogman came up from below deck.

"Ah! Señora, for you. The grand opera of the sea. Hear Casals? It's a tactic Lord Nelson would want to conduct for his Majesty King of England. The Spanish Lady Maria Louisa, Picasso, and the Water Bottle Player are sending into the sky canister after canister of glaring, deafening fireworks above the bay from Port Vells in the West."

"Look. More fireworks from Blava Cove behind us."

"Si. Darth Vader and the 'Head' are setting those fireworks off from the East. They are computerized—Dali's design."

"Come in. This is the Clown."

We were among crews and boats reaching for the next marker across the opening of the bay. The king's maxi, off our right quarter, was going to pass us. "Hello, Red Head," I said.

"Dana Poole, I am on Cape Regana and can see all of you. May I ruffle your back to get you to move? If you do not perform now, you'll be covered in smoke, spuds, and spume and you will not be able to see."

"Clown, we are moving. Check the roads for squads of soldiers and look offshore for naval vessels with surface search radar. Clown, I'll be with you shortly. Over."

I felt hot in my wet suit when Colón placed the missile launcher on my shoulder. His Majesty the King of Spain, about nine hundred feet to our right, evaluated the luff and curvature of his glistening mainsail. Ahead of him sailed the boats we had passed through and those we allowed to pass on. Officials and observing yacht club members on motor launches passed offshore to our left.

The missile launcher weighed at least fifty pounds. It was good I had practiced. Beyond the king, about four and a half miles, I saw the old city of Palma and envisioned Owen talking on the transmitter-receiver. God almighty! He's in my line of fire!

The frogman hit my left shoulder. "Look up! Look up!"

"Where did that come from?" It was the black helicopter and the pilot saw me! His side door slid open. The wind whipped.

I had no choice. I changed guidance system to optical laser beam-rider, lifted, and squeezed the trigger. I knew I had to leave the sight accurately on the pilot because the missile remains in the center of the laser until it hits the plane. They were going to machine-gun us down. I had separated my legs.

It took time. I hit the deck. Debris from the plane went everywhere. Five hundred feet is not far from up there. Our 'geny' sail was cut apart. Colón jumped below.

He discarded the long stem roses from around the shafts. He fletched yellow feathers into grooves. He took a minute to clean off the cool soil from around the arrowheads. I received the compound bow from below. A couple of seconds later, from against his chest, Colón handed me, gently, a special arrow with nitroglycerin the equivalent of a small shot glass sealed into the arrow's broad head where three swing hunting blades would have been attached.

I took it gently because twenty pounds of pressure against the chiseled point tip and I would never see Ireland and my children again.

I looked to the king. The Moor was right. Only the tactician and Juan Carlos remained in the cockpit. The crew showed black heads and red shoulders in the water. I stepped to the deck next to the cabin roof. Colón carried up two more special arrows against his body. I presumed if the boat jerked and if he fell, he could cushion the fall with his body by contorting, squirming, never allowing the arrow heads to hit the solid plastic boat.

I positioned myself windward behind the mainsail. My feet were among the rigging lines on the cabin roof leading to the cockpit. I had peeked around the leech of the mainsail and judged a spot—a batten pocket—near the top that I needed to guide my arrow to land on the king's deck. In the posture of Robin Hood, I waited for the pitch, roll, and yaw of the boat to be exactly as when I picked my spot on the leech. What was his roll and yaw? "Damn."

I let an arrow go. It moved at three hundred feet per second. It went long, over his deck. Hell, let them go. There were too many variables. I released number two and number three arrow just a little differently. They blasted the king, his yacht, and his loyal subject off the earth!

A 120-millimeter recoilless gun placed a tracer across our bow. The white, generated smoke came toward us. Seeing and hearing the ceaseless fireworks, the cacophonous music, and the racing fleet scrambling in all directions, I had a feeling of relief, of momentary success.

"Señora, here are two more arrows."

The sound of recoilless weapon air pressure would be repeated if I didn't do something.

I turned aft and saw the black frigate bearing down on us. The ship's rectangular bridge and cabin magnified as its steel bow plowed blue water into white waves.

Aiming very high, I toasted the women of the world against suppression and the bow and arrow, a weapon disfavored by the military. One-half of a mile would be a record. With all my strength and the power of a compound bow, I let go. The equivalent of a shot glass of nitroglycerin eliminated the replica of a post-World War II naval craft to the waters and seabed of Palma Bay.

The brown Indian passed with his starched feathers streaming. White smoke engulfed us. Visibility measured in feet. I actually had cleared the way for the speedboat. I had no idea what the Indian and Visigoth would have done facing a frigate.

The frogman already released the transom davit lines. A blue-green, black Yamaha SUV 1200 water bike sat in our mild wake. It was twelve feet-seven inches long and weighed nine hundred pounds. The original shiny colors of maroon and white had been changed to thick radar absorbing paint and its metal replaced with composite as much as possible. It performed well and was fun to handle in rough water. It stayed put.

Along the coasts, I would confront undertow, rebounding waves, eddies, and changing currents in dangerous, uncharted ways. The water bike had great compartments for extra fuel, food, warmers, charts, radios, global positioning equipment, and handheld radar. I jumped on the three-person seat and faced digital instruments. Pulling my goggles from behind my neck around and over my eyes, I blasted off! I read fifty-two miles per hour. No one would get in my way.

Owen

"She's coming out of the smoke screen. The other frigate is in it. Can you hear me, Clown? Over."

"Yes, 0. *Dana* 00 is safe now. She'll hide in the coves, caves, gorges, and French calanques. She has only a one hundred foot coastal window from radar. She'll travel between Menorca and Mallorca. With patience, in and out bursts of speed, and night navigation, she'll avoid surface radar detection. France, England, and home it will be for her, Sir."

"Are you ex-British navy, Clown? You talk like it. Keep in touch with her for as long as you can."

"Aye, Sir. To Cap de Formentor."

"Be careful. There are six thousand troops in the Balearics. Over and out."

"Come in. Ha. Owen. It is you, Señor Owen?"

"Yes, Miguel, where are you?"

"Muelle de la Lonja, loading platform by the market, below you to your, ha, right. My Mallorcan friends dry their nets strung along this cement and beach. We repair them today. How is Mimi?"

219

"She picked up the Visigoth and has just come out the southwest cloud of smoke in a Ski-Doo. Her blonde hair's blazing. The wake is ten times the length of her personal watercraft. They look like a young couple enjoying speed on the water."

"Can you see the Indian, Owen?"

"He blew up the smoke generator, the speed boat, and added to the fleet's dispersion. He joined the frogman who used an arrow to detonate the Clipper. They are swimming underwater to caves near Port Nous where the king used to keep his boat. Miguel, through my telescope I see the black frigate coming up behind Mimi Meninges. It's working!"

"Ha. Everything will be in order. Lady Poole has to be nine miles in the opposite direction."

"Yes. She is now in hiding until tonight."

"Señor. *Grande!* Si?"

"It is not over yet."

"Ha. It is. Come down. Above me is a nice restaurant. Live music. You see our hottest equipment."

I told Miguel to dispose of the radio receiver-transmitters, in case the police started monitoring sport and family ultra-high frequency transmissions. It may be the end.

Owen

Las Ramblas was here in Palma, not Barcelona. Don't move and no one will catch you. A "Black Thunder" luxury edition powerboat capable of over seventy-five miles an hour docked within walking distance. It was sent right from Missouri, USA.

Diego, on deck, wound up practicing his pitching motion. His knee went to his chin, and his hamstrings shined. The deadpan sombrero dog pointed to the team on shore.

The bride cried under a pile of nets in front and below me. The Mercedes driver, a weight lifter from Basque country with his driver's cap reversed, sat on top of her. She was a liability. Darth Vader, the "Head," the water Jar Player, Casals, Sombrero, Dali, all fishermen now, walked up and down the drying nets, some sitting on stools to make repairs, but all waiting. They knew it might be days before the new "Black Thunder" would take them to the *paseo* of Barcelona's *Ramblas*.

On the Autopista de Llevant, the airport road, and Avinguda Gabriel Roca, many vehicles and jeeps displayed soldiers. A state of emergency existed on the island.

A few tables to my left under the giant, white umbrella sat the Spanish Lady—her parasol spinning redundantly over her left shoulder. The lace over her hair and pearls around her neck worried me. She could be robbed. Across from her, young Picasso smoked, boasted, and contemplated seduction.

"Another Pepsi max, *por favor*."

Miguel closed the door of an old van next to the drying nets and buoys. He might come up to say good-bye. It's better if he doesn't. He is right. It's over.

Owen

I thought of Poole. She rode the supercharged Yamaha as if it were a filly. Her mind was a quagmire when she wasn't working. If you got in it, you were engorged, swollen, then deflated by cuts and gashes and eventually a buzz saw. She would be in a gorge now, camouflaged, starry-eyed, cautious, looking at pitted rocks or gazing up the limestone cliffs for helicopters. She was in constant competition. What brought us close? What separated us? I wondered what she did for peaceful enjoyment.

There may come a point when she might not know what to do. She intensely disliked this trait in others, as if she had it herself. It called for self-hate or inward aggression and made her the consummate murderer who is angered by unacknowledged feelings of insecurity or hopelessness. I became concerned, as if her time may have come.

The piano music, "The Ritual Fire Dance" by Falla, played in my brain. Poole will have help at Toulouse University. Port-

Vendres or Argelês-on the sea, onward to Perpignan, Narbonne, and Toulouse—that was her escape route. Good luck to you, Poole. So long. Enjoy youth at Toulouse. Dance on tables. You like being alone, yet you like beautiful, young people for what they offer. You'll deserve the release.

Owen in the USA

State Street, Ann Arbor resonated football and more football, people and more people. Luckily, I got a booth in a coffee shop. I put a coin in the jukebox. It was late October.

Two months had passed and all I did was talk and talk standing in front of an amphitheater to students who actually listened. I liked the new generation. The questions and feedback made teaching more enjoyable. But, that's all I did.

Poole sent a letter to a post office box. She wrote that she had called her second husband and told him to screw himself. She, Mabel, and the children moved to Cork. The Dublin archery team romped Cork's butt and now she lived in a large London apartment. She also wrote she hadn't heard from the Cardinal either, but didn't care because she was paid up front. She wrote that she waited for the next message to Oxford University at a college I wasn't aware was part of the business. She said she also waited for me. "Um."

The coffee shop was no Agut D'Avignon—a fine Catalan restaurant off *Las Ramblas*. There wasn't any insurance for what was going on. Only if something has no value can you get insurance. Additionally, my girls said the fifty cycle government-approved cassette tapes bought on *Ramblas* wouldn't play clearly in their videocassette recorder.

The Pope and Cardinal blocked my access to the main computer. I was on the outside. Desuetude prevailed.

I moved the coffee cup to the right on the pearly Formica tabletop. I spread the newspaper open to an international page. There in clear print: King Juan Carlos will visit the Queen Sofia Music Academy in Madrid. The king and queen will travel to attend the signing of a comprehensive Peru-Ecuador agreement that ends the bitter border dispute that last flared into war in 1995.

I pressed my lips together and hummed the melody breathing from the jukebox. The base guitar beat in four quarter time, "Follow - all my heart, swallow - all my tears; oooOo oooOo oooOo 0000. oooOo 'tic-tac-' 'tic-tac-'...."

The saxophone blew. You can't win all the time. One must win the critical points at the crucial moment. "Malaguena" played from a piano in an adjacent tenement. What stays the same? What changes? What's my next move? □

About the Author

Richard F. Jarmain began writing short stories part-time in 1997, but his first published book was *Poet's Modern Poet "Human Exposure"* in 2003. It's a serious book of poems that has brought him notoriety.

Writer's Digest was impressed by Richard's commitment to produce this fine collection of poems. The range of subjects from relationships to loneliness and the small poems with enduring strength have been given editorial praise.

The short stories were put on the back burner as Richard wrote his first novel, Saltwater Run, published in 2005. It's the exciting informative story of a teacher working on a yacht during summer break and it's finding a warm reception from lovers of the sea and lovers of adventure.

When Richard studied at Niagara University he took an elective course on short stories. What impressed him most was that, as in everyone, creativity existed in his being and that it could be expressed. This pleased him. His creativity was best realized in writing. It was a way of being useful and entertaining. Both he and his readers have benefited ever since.

Very shortly, another book will follow this *Short, Long, and Longer Short Stories*. Watch for *Thirteen Stories*! It will be worth the brief wait!

Printed in the United States
28271LVS00001B/103-126

9 781418 400699